Song for the Dead

Song for the Dead

a novel

Andrew Cusick

GREEN CITY
BOOKS

Green City Books

For more information, contact Green City Books:

editors@greencitybooks.com

Published 2025

Published in the United States of America

ISBN: 9781963101102

Paperback $16.95 US | $23.99 CAD

First Edition

designed by Isaac Peterson

cover art by Isaac Peterson

Library of Congress cataloging-in-publication data has been applied for.

Part I

1.

After he leaves, I find the note Mason rested on his bedroom pillow—*I AM NOT GONE.*

An hour later, I watch the police rummage through his desk, cherry-pick the pipe and rolling papers, the empty bottle of Rolling Rock, the note they don't let me see again. I sit on the couch downstairs, watching TV as they question Mom and time slows down and the TV runs stories on all the whispers of violence and pain and ugliness and Mom comes back into the house, first whispering about a surveillance video and a boy jumping from the side of a bridge and then she is frantic, *where is he, where is he, where did he go* and then she is screaming, and in that moment, I know the summer's story will be about death.

Jersey Shore. First of July.

A few days pass and more videos from the restaurants across the bay and they all but tell us that he's dead and that he did it himself and that the body will wash up at some point and that when it does maybe it's best that nobody sees it.

There's debate back and forth—Mom and the authorities and some of Mom's distant relatives who we don't see any more and even a little bit of me: what if he comes home, what if he didn't die, what if this is just a bad dream, but first it's hours and then it's days and then it's closing on a week and Mom says one night that death is a thing that keeps happening until it becomes a thing that happened, and that same night she's on the phone with a funeral director.

They hold a service for him in Holmdel at the big Victorian church that we both were baptized in. The organ drones and the air periodically sputters with sobs and the sound of an off-key Leonard Cohen cover and that cheap cold smell of processed air. The priest talks about "unfortunate choices" and he says that human beings lean into the light when things are darkest and that's what faith is. He says that goodness is there in the dark and the ugly things and that we must look for the good inside the bad. They tell us to put the things that he loved inside of the coffin and so we put a pair of guitar picks and sand from the beach on Second Ave and one of the leashes from his surfboard, *Nevermind* and *Tim* and *Wildflowers* and pictures of Mom and I, and Mom says, when the service is over, that love doesn't come in things or pictures.

Staring at the ocean a few hours later.

"What do we do now?" Mom asks.

"I don't know."

"When they find him, I think we should scatter his ashes. I think that's what he would want."

"Mason's ashes."

"Yeah."

"Where?"

"The ocean."

"Why?"

"I think he'd like it."

A beat.

"They haven't found him yet, Ma."

"They will soon."

"I mean . . . it was him, right?"

"Yes," she says, more softly. "It was Mason."

I AM NOT GONE

We both stare out at the water without saying anything and the waves lap onto the beach on Fourth and when the storm clouds roll in, we both sit there not speaking and watching the dry lightning move like spiders across gray clouds. Mom stands on the edge of the water, her frame small against the backdrop of the storm moving in off the coast, the black glasses on the bridge of her nose, her tan skin whiter than it's ever been since his leaving.

At home I watch Mom stare at the cabinet, jars of pasta sauce and thin boxes of fettuccine and rigatoni. It feels horrific: the idea of preparing dinner for a smaller table. She turns to me and shakes her head and then we're back in the car.

We're at the Tropicana Diner and the woman serving reads off the specials and says that the key lime pie is good and that we should try it. Mom gets a steak Caesar and picks at it and I get an order of onion rings and a soda. Afterwards the woman reminds us about the pie and so we both order a slice and have a few bites.

On the car ride home, Mom turns on a Springsteen song and sings along. She says he wrote the song about loss and love and that *Magic* is the best Springsteen album even if nobody agrees with her. She says Mason used to come home from surfing and stand in the rain and she remembers listening to the album and watching him stand outside and wondering what he was thinking, and she says she'll always miss wondering what he was thinking or even just watching him stand in the rain.

The beat of your heart the beat of your heart

The Boss sings us home.

I don't sleep much and when I do it's a tumble into nightmares and when I wake up I wonder for a second if I've just been comatose this whole time and when I run down the hallway my brother will be standing there with his arm on the door looking at me with a towel around his waist and a toothbrush rammed inside of his mouth and a bottle of Heineken he just finished in his other hand and that shit-eating grin on his face telling me about government PsyOps and how fluoride in water is enough to keep our teeth clean and we don't actually need to brush as often as we do and my mom will be standing behind him shaking her head the way she always does when Mason is being himself and she'll say something like "don't be such a weirdo" and we'll sit at the dinner table later that night with the pizza that we ordered and my mom will let us take a sip of her beer even if she knows how we've snuck it before and how we sneak it most weekends but instead of all that, instead of any of that, I wander down the hallway in the dark in the blue dim light of the night and find Mom inside of her room on the floor and the sounds are like something out of a movie like she's being hacked to pieces slashed and torn and dissected and gutted and any of that because that's all I can imagine all I can equate all I can conjure to come up with how much pain I'd rather be in how much physical horrible suffering I'd rather endure than watching her face buried in the hue of the red carpet that she bought with us one rainy January when we had nothing to do and I want to go to him I want to die and be with him I just want to see him again and die and be with him again just die again and again . . .

X

The next night at practice, the sun setting over the trees in Thompson Park, the sound of crickets, the air heavy. Coach Taylor slaps me in the face, adjusts his MOC cap.

"Time to recover," he says. Taylor is tall and thick, bigger than big, his face tan and seared with spaghetti veins and flushed skin pumped full of Michelob Ultra, nachos, cigarettes. He has been the coach since the dawn of time and an incredibly successful, abrasive one at that.

We do recovery runs after hard workouts or long runs, all the ones that kick the shit out of you, the ones that leave you sitting in your car in as much A/C as possible, swilling half-Gatorade, half-water jugs and swallowing salt tablets and trying not to puke. Pace goes out the window and you're meant to end the thing feeling better than you started and hopefully by the next day, ready to tackle another bigger meaner run or a workout or a tempo or a progression. Taylor is old and plodding now, but by all accounts ran as a kid even if I don't really believe it. He has his name listed on the all-time list at the back, a list that he keeps in file cabinets wedged into the back of the tiny locker room the school allocates us each year, shared usually with some JV program like the Archers.

The team stretches on the asphalt and the girls from Manasquan run past us and a couple of steps down the path they start to giggle, most of them girls the boys on the team have traded around. The team watches them go, ogling them without speaking, weird slack-jawed zombies. I watch Chase—his right knee pointed up to the sky, his ass on the ground. He turns to me and locks eyes and raises the middle finger on his right hand. Chase is blond-haired, shorter than I am, a little heavier. Most distance runners have that gangly Gumby look—Chase is something like an exception. I'm the fastest returner on the team since Richie Benedict graduated, and Chase is right behind me.

"Who's taking the pace?" I ask.

"I don't know. I can do it."

"You always do it. I can take over for a day."

He shrugs. "Doesn't matter to me." He pushes himself up from the concrete. "On the line in five," he says, walking to the start.

We start the run a few minutes later, moving off the asphalt, through the dirt path and into the woods, up through roots and rocks and hills and trails, the heat of the summer trapped inside of the Jersey jungle inside of the park. Chase stays up for ten or fifteen minutes and I get bored so I pick up the pace, bit by bit, until Chase's breathing turns ragged and he tells me to slow down. I ignore him and twenty minutes in I try to drop his ass but he pushes and stays with me. The rest of the team separates into another pack behind us and then it's just both of us breathing and moving like wind through the trees, the crash of our Asics the only sound on the wet ground. He doesn't talk much and I don't ask many questions and I don't want many questions asked and maybe that's why we're a good pair. I'm cruising, setting sun beating down on tan skin and sweat flying off. It hurts, not as much as last week, but it hurts.

So I run hard and I run harder and I run the hardest I've ever run at practice, and time just sort of vanishes into my own thoughts.

Seventy minutes later, I close in 5:14, way too fucking fast, and I'm sprawled out on the asphalt with my legs splayed out, hamstrings knotted and my right ankle pulsing. Chase comes up to me and punches me in the arm.

"What was that?" he asks.

"Felt good."

"Yeah did it feel stupid too? " he says.

I rub my ankle again and try to rub the knot out but it doesn't really seem to work. I listen to the rest of the team carrying on about trying to get laid at a party in Manasquan at a summer mansion rented out by some Wall Street hobgoblin. My eyes stay on my phone—Mason's face illuminated in the background. Chase puts his hand on my shoulder. I push it off.

"Want to get fucked up?" I ask.

"Yeah," he says. "Yeah, I do."

X

Underneath the boardwalk in Asbury Park, passing a bar of chocolate mushrooms back and forth, microdosing and listening to the band bleating out from the Stone Pony. Chase giggles the entire time.

"What're they called?" he asks.

"I think Vroom. Like the street."

"Oh yeah. They from around here?"

"Born and raised. Jed went to St. Rose. Bass player."

"Where'd you get the shrooms from?"

"You remember Elijah?"

"That fucking weirdo we met at the party."

"What a weird motherfucker. Dude spent the first night we met him telling us we all lived in a simulation and there were electric bugs in our skin tracking our movements. Who says hello like that?"

"A weird motherfucker," he says. "Like you said."

"Nice guy, I guess."

Chase cocks his head toward the sound of the music.

"You going to keep playing?" he asks.

"I guess."

"It'll be tough without him, I imagine."

"Yeah."

"Maybe Jake will fill in."

"Can we not?"

"Sorry."

We get too stoned so we both stop talking for a while and then we're lying with our heads on the sand and our eyes on the stars.

"Dec."

"Yeah."

"I know you don't want to talk . . ."

"It's alright. We can talk."

"Do you miss him?"

"Yeah."

"It's okay if you don't want to talk."

"I said we can talk."

"I wish I knew him better."

"Me too."

"Sorry."

"It's okay."

A beat.

"I could've asked him to go for a run. Go to a show. Smoke some weed. It doesn't matter. Anything."

Another beat.

"I'm sorry he's gone," Chase says.

"Missing," I say. "Not gone. Missing."

In the background, the band plays a Pixies song I recognize and I focus on the high and the sound of the waves. When the band stops, Chase gets his phone out and we watch some Snap stories from some girls and he shows me some naked chicks that sent him pics unprompted. I float away into the dark.

ᛯ

I'm too cooked to drive home so I catch an Uber and Chase asks me if he can stay. I live in one of those oversized, blue-slatted modular homes in Belmar a few blocks from the beach. I can hear the ocean from the windows and the floors are all hardwood and there's glib little signs that say things like "Beach House Rules" and an outdoor shower and sometimes there's sand on the floor and in my bed and all the bennies from New York stare at my house on Saturday nights and point and talk about the townies that live here. Dad had sent us some money before he died, and then when he died, we got more.

"You're late," Mom says when we walk in, her eyes on the television set, pictures of scrolling sets of numbers and stock prices and question marks, a torn American flag waving in the wind. She gestures toward the clock: 11:07. She locks eyes with both of us.

"Sorry, Ma," I say.

"Nice to see you, Chase."

"Nice to see you too."

Chase excuses himself to the bathroom. I stand in the kitchen with her, and she points to an urn sitting above the fireplace.

"It's for his ashes. When he washes up," she says.

I walk up to the urn and run my hand along the metal.

"If he washes up, Ma."

We are still for a moment, quiet inside the house. She stands up and walks over to the liquor cabinet and pulls out a tumbler and a bottle of bourbon and pours the bourbon and sits down wordlessly. For a second, I just watch her there, holding the glass and not drinking from it, and then I feel like she doesn't want me there anymore so I leave.

In the basement later, Chase and I both drinking lime seltzer and eating Cool Ranch Doritos and watching the remake of *The Hills Have Eyes*, the scene where the dad gets crucified and burned alive. Chase mutters something under his breath as the dad is screaming but I don't catch it.

Later he comes upstairs and we both get down into our boxers and I crawl into bed and leave the left side open for him.

"I'll just take the floor," he says, grabbing a pillow. He vanishes from sight. I lie awake and wait for him to start snoring but he never does and I imagine him staring at the ceiling and waiting too.

2.

THE NEXT MORNING CHASE LEAVES before I wake up. My body hurts. I scroll through my phone and stare at Mason's Instagram posts. I look at some of his old TikTok videos. *A boy dives off the motel roof into the pool after prom. Everybody cheers.*

"Hey hey, check it out . . ."

Tumbling through the air into the water—

I sit up in bed and stand and my ankle sends a slice through my nerves for a second. I rub the spot in between the bone and my shin, tibia or fibula or whatever. It doesn't get better.

Downstairs, Mom finds me at the breakfast nook, computer in hand. She is dressed in some kind of flowing blue robe and her hair looks electric and scattered and her eyes are bloodshot. She walks over to the coffee machine and smacks at it a few times, rummages through the Folgers inside the cupboard, sends things crashing hither and thither, sighs when she has to fill the reservoir with water. Then she's over near me, leaning over, staring at the computer screen in front of me, the open document that I started the night after he died, a series of scribbles at best.

Leaning into the Dark

That's the title. I don't have much of anything besides it, and I don't even know what a book is supposed to look like. But I've been writing stories about him, putting him down, little sketches. I don't have a plot, a framework, any of that, but I have him, alive, on the page. I can put him inside the story, and I can give him things to do, people to see. I can give him words to say, things to do, people to meet, barbeques to attend, someone to fall in love with, children to have, stupid bills to pay, and dumb little backyard gardens to forget to water.

"What is this?" Mom asks, her hand on my shoulder. She smells like coffee, last night's bourbon, the perfume she always used to wear on Christmas.

"Just something."

"Just something?"

"Yeah."

"About Mason?"

"Yeah."

Her voice picks up.

"Writing about him?"

"Trying."

She rummages through the cabinets some more.

"Is it any good?"

"It's just a few pages."

"So is it any good?"

"It's a real piece of shit, Ma."

"I don't believe you."

"I don't know." I rub my eyes. "I can't sleep really. I just think about it over and over. So I just started writing it down."

"I can't sleep either."

She finds what she's looking for inside the cupboard, pulls out a pink bag with a hemp symbol on the front of it.

"This helps," she says, pulling out a pair of orange gummies.

"Think you're supposed to take them before bed," I say.

"Yeah, well, like I said—nobody's sleeping around here anyway. Might as well sleep during the day."

"I keep having these awful dreams about him."

"Every night," she says. "I just see him on that bridge."

"Me too."

She pops a pair of gummies into her mouth, starts chewing. I watch her open the fridge and fumble for a glass of orange juice and she shoots that down before fumbling over to the Keurig and taking her cup.

"I am . . . I was—they say you should talk about him in the past tense, that it's healthier. I was . . . I was his mother. I should've been there. I should've—I bandaged up his knees when he'd fall. I cleaned up bloody noses during the winter. I held his hand when they set his shoulder. Where was I in that moment? When he died? Where was I?"

"You were here."

"I'm his mother. Where was I when he died? Did he think about me? Was I the last thing he saw behind his eyes?"

A beat.

"We don't know everything yet, Mom," I say.

She shakes her head and then the words hang in the air for a moment and then there's nothing. She walks away and starts to make breakfast. She cracks two eggs and then pauses, turns to look at me, and cracks two more. She unzips a pack of maple bacon and throws it on to a cast iron and turns on the flame. I stare at her in motion and wonder what she's thinking. The sizzle grows slowly, and I catch the smell on the air.

When I'm eating, I'm tapping out drum beats on the kitchen marble and Mom asks if I'm going to keep playing and I say that I don't know.

"You should. Go play. Put some noise in this house. Can't take the silence," she says.

She walks away from the kitchen table and up to the liquor cabinet where she takes out a small bottle of amaretto and pours it into her coffee. She places the coffee on top of the psych textbooks she's left splayed out all over the countertop. Mom has been a psych professor over at Monmouth since I was born.

"The fucking silence," she says emphatically, nearly spilling some of the coffee on the hardcovers.

I'm in the basement on the drum set smacking away, starting with some kind of "Streets of Philadelphia" thing before attacking the cymbals and smacking the heel of my feet as hard as I can, trying to break the bass drum, hitting the snare over and over and over and over . . .

I'm outside Mason's door sitting on the edge of the doorframe and listening inside wondering when he is going to come home. I put my ear to the wood and close my eyes and think that maybe if I close my eyes for long enough, I can shift the fabric of time and reset the clock.

I AM NOT GONE

I'm on the boardwalk soaked in sweat, eyes on the storm out at sea, my ankle throbbing, staring at the text that just came through.

Meet me at the South Pavilion @ 6?

Jake, Mason's closest friend and our bandmate since we were kids. Jake was on the lead vocals and rhythm, Mason played lead, and I was the drummer. Slim played the bass, for better or worse.

I park the car and sit on the edge of the boardwalk. I watch clouds move over the ocean rapidly, like something out of a silent film. This is the 732 at its most postcardesque.

All of us are from the geographic armpit of the Jersey Shore—Monmouth County. The county has its fair share of poverty and ghettos but, truth be told, much of it is an extended summer Carnival Americana: it exists twelve months of the year with the sole purpose of fueling those summer months. If you cut down Ocean Avenue from Highlands to Pt. Pleasant from May to September, it was an endless sequence of unaffordable real estate, bars overflowing with white boy frat heroes, flashing neon and circulating greens of various beach clubs, fairs, and concerts in Asbury Park: heroic places like the Stone Pony, Asbury Lanes, the Wonder Bar, rites of passage for any rock band worth their weight in gold. In the last few years, for whatever reason, Monmouth County has endured a seemingly endless onslaught of dead teenagers. There was no reason for any of this: most of the ones who went missing came from a life of privilege and basic goodness; on the surface, at least, their families were well put together and they went to the right schools and they were on the right teams and they said the right things and they dated the right girls and guys and they smoked the right weed and drank the right beer and they put the right things up on TikTok. But, for whatever reason, there was a creeping sadness that had infected the area, an area that, like many of its recently deceased inhabitants, seemed all but perfect on the outside. Mason had been infected. That's what pulled him away.

A few hours later, a couple of Coronas snuck into Solo cups, the beach cruiser cops giving us a handful of nods, Jake and I sitting on the edge of the pavilion, where the sand meets the boardwalk. Jake is older than me—as old as Mason was, twenty years old—halfway into college. They'd met years ago when they were kids and they bonded over the absentee dads and they both played music and fell in love with each other that way. Some nights they'd let me tag along and a few times they let me jam with them in Jake's garage where sand on your feet would slough off onto the cold concrete and the sand would stay there through the fall and the dead of winter and remind you how the summer never died if you believed it enough. Eventually I just became the drummer in their band, and we all became some kind of unit.

The boy pulls me out of the house quickly, practically pushing me down the veranda onto the grass, into the car that's already parked out front.

"Let's go, go, go," the boy says, giggling.

"What the fuck?" I'm shouting. Jake starts laughing as he pulls away, hard and fast, the water balloon launcher that we've been using as a shelling operation now wedged in between his legs.

Jake was taller than Mason and handsome, features were less mysterious and vague, and he looked like some kind of Aryan poster boy but he was always solid and decent and reliable and I guess that's why Mason latched onto him so much—some kind of constant in Mason's ever-shifting equation.

Jake and I are on the boardwalk sharing a bench, both of our feet on the ledge in front of us. Some late beach stragglers wander around the sand in front of us, families and teenage couples making out and past six now, all the bennies and tourists who don't want to pay the money and now can sneak some food and booze onto the beach without being bothered too much.

"You alright?" he asks.

"No," I say.

Jake takes a sip from his beer and speaks up. "I canceled the show. Canceled it. Don't . . . without him, don't have enough practice yet."

"You'll be fine where he was," I say. "And we can practice. If we still want to do the band."

"I want the band to survive," he says. "Do you?"

"I think."

"I mean, we can just play a few shows and try it out. It's not the end of the world."

"Maybe it'll be good for me," I say.

"Do you want to talk?" he says.

"I just want people to stop asking me that. Do I want to talk? No, I don't want to talk. Of course I'm not okay. Just fuck off—everybody."

"Sorry," he says, quiet.

"Just nothing. I'd rather nothing. No words. Just quiet and leave-me-the-fuck-alone. Sorry. I'm just over it. I don't want to talk about it. I don't want to talk about anything."

A beat.

"What did it mean?" I ask.

"What did what mean?"

"His suicide note. *I AM NOT GONE.* What the fuck does that mean?"

"I don't know," Jake says.

"I just keep thinking about it," I say. "And don't call it a suicide note. They haven't even found the body yet."

He takes a sip of his beer. The waves crash onto the shore. Somebody honks a horn from one of the streets behind us. The smell of rain on the air.

"I'm trying to write something," I say. "Something about him. I saw something online that says writing is something like therapy."

"Your brother used to just scribble all the time. Song lyrics. Poems. Whatever. He'd write them on paper he carried around. Bar napkins. Whatever he could find. It was like his mind was overflowing all the time."

A beat.

"Did you know?" he asks abruptly, eyes on his beer.

"What?"

"I mean . . . did Mason say anything? Did you have any hint?"

"That morning, he pulled me into his room and showed me a new song. Then he was gone."

"'Song for the Dead,'" Jake says.

"Yeah. That's it."

"Probably the best thing he ever wrote," he says.

"The last thing he ever wrote."

"He thought that song was special. He thought he had a hit on his hands. He sent me a recording of it. Just him and his guitar. He talked to me about it the morning he died. We were surfing."

"It was pretty. It was really pretty," I say.

"Like I said . . . he thought he had a hit."

"Maybe he did. In a different life," I say.

I let that hang in the air for a while, finish the Coronas. The clouds swim in the distance.

"Maybe we should try to do something with it," Jake says.

"With what?"

"His song."

"Like?"

"I don't know. It had that thing."

"What thing?"

"Where you've heard it before, even if you haven't. That quality. That . . . thing."

"You want to try to record it?" I ask.

"Yeah," he says. "I mean . . . I still remember it. He showed me the whole song. We can put it down. It can become his song. At least some good will come out of it." He says the last part quickly like he's realizing what the words mean as he's saying them. I don't really respond though.

"Yeah," I say, muted. "Maybe."

"It could be like a tribute . . . you know," he offers.

"I don't know."

"I mean, we don't have to."

"I said I don't know."

"Okay," he says.

A few streaks of dry lightning move across the sky. There is a grayness and a stillness and something melancholy and something magical splashing through the air. I close my eyes and listen to the sound of the water. I listen for the sound of Mason's voice over the water, behind us, a hand on a shoulder, *come back to me, come back to me.*

I open my eyes. The moonlight on the water pulses and flashes. People here and there gather on the line where the water and the sand meet and stare at the light.

X

That night I cry myself to sleep, my mind resting on some little sign, some lever I could've flipped to get him back, beer in his hand, girl on his shoulder, some light switch that I left unturned, some stray remark I could've reeled in, whatever it may have been to bring him back.

He was up and down all the time, if I am being honest. That's what made him beautiful and magical and that's what made him difficult and ugly. It could be the span of twenty minutes and sometimes his ups were so high they teetered on mania and his lows were never *that* low and that was the part, in retrospect, that bothers me the most—that the signs *weren't* actually there, that he was just a heartbroken, confused kid, just like all of us. Yeah, maybe I could point to a song on a Twitter profile or an offhand comment at a backyard BBQ, but truth be told, he was just a puzzle I couldn't crack, the same kid who'd spend all night smoking weed and dropping acid and making me watch the Coppola cut (the third one) of *Apocalypse Now* and then stay up and read *Tropic of Capricorn* and then make me read it too and he'd tell me that sometimes he thought he was from Mars, that he couldn't understand people, and they couldn't understand him, and I remember when he asked Mom if he was adopted and she looked at him like he was fucking nuts. I remember the way he used to react to the world around him: any shooting or bombing or death or anything that was wrong and terrible and broken seemed to send an actual shockwave through him, like despite all the bloviating and loudness that perpetuated him, he was just made of chocolate, wanting to know why people threw rocks at each other at the park as a young kid, perpetually sitting on those wood chips they sprawl out on half-rusted playgrounds. I remember watching a movie with Mel Gibson in it, something about lonely boy crackpot conspiracies, and I remember Mason crying for no reason at all, he must've been ten years old, saying that he just felt so bad watching it and he didn't want to watch it anymore. The next day he made me wrestle for about three hours straight until he finally pinned me. Two days before he kills himself, he puts up Facebook posts about children in Palestine being shredded to pieces.

It visits on me too sometimes: this feeling, the same feeling I know Mason had at the end, the feeling he must've wanted people to know about. Every once in a while, I feel it—that *beyond* nothingness, that hollowness, that feeling of emptiness that's so cold and black and terrible I could imagine doing anything, *anything*, to run from it forever. Mason used to say that the purpose of life is whatever we do that stops us from killing ourselves and I just don't know what to make of that anymore.

I hear the phone buzzing on the counter, text messages from Chase or more messages from people trying to make themselves feel better by making me feel better. I hear the loudness of our mom downstairs, opening and closing kitchen cabinets, cleaning, doing whatever. What I want is that silence back: the silent violence that people inflict on each other, fights with Mom and Mason, fights with Mason and I, the incessant nagging annoyance of being alive, not the looping agony of the last few weeks. I crawl into the pillow as far as I can.

Sometimes it's everywhere at once: how Mase used to play music on his headphones and the way he let me lean in on car rides to share one, the sound of the distorted fuzz of the Ibanez rattling the floors, the open mic shows he put on at Asbury Lanes, the punk rock cover of "Mercy Street," the smell of the Marlboros he ashed in half-filled Miller Lite cans, the seventies porno mags caked in yellow and rot that he found in the basement and hid underneath his bed, the way he refused to wash his hair during the summer, the flashes of hushed blues and reds outside the front door the night he died.

Tuesdays are for workouts—up at the school track usually around six p.m. I go to a local boys' school called Institute High. Most of the Irish Catholics and Italian Catholics and Episcopalians, the non-dairy Catholics, funnel in either here or the local public schools, but attendance has been down the last few years at the Institute, as it's more colloquially known: I guess there's not a lot of love for the Catholic thing these days, with my own vivid recollections of an old wrinkly priest they canned for standing too close to the boys locker rooms after cross country practice trying to sneak glimpses of dropped towels, wet skin, the occasional swinging dick. The whole team meets up at the Institute track and we pass around stories and most of the kids either avoid me or try too hard to actively talk to me, are you okay, your brother seemed great, I heard you have a pretty good fake can you buy me some booze.

"Is Taylor coming?" one of the rising freshmen asks.

"Taylor doesn't come to track workouts," another voice answers. This is Timmy Carter, stud of the year, handsome fourth man on the XC squad who thinks he's the first man and has limited time left before he's sitting on the wrong end of an Irish bar asking them to turn the jukebox louder.

He misses too many days hungover and he doesn't really give a shit about much to begin with and he comes from a family of uber-loaded miscreants anyway. I remember him being good as a kid, but then he just stopped caring and got sucked into the coked-up Goldman Sachs wannabe crowd.

"How do we log the pace without him here? He didn't tell the frosh—" the frosh asks.

Carter interrupts. "Figure it out."

I pull the frosh aside before the run begins. "Take the first few in 6:40. Drop down to 5:45-ish by the end if you can. It's hot. Don't panic if you can't. And don't listen to Carter, ever."

Taylor only calls practices Monday, Wednesday, Friday, 6:30 p.m. at Thompson Park—miles and miles and miles through trails and loops and hills and ticks and bugs and scratches and scrapes and blood. Tuesday nights the team meets at dusk up at the track to do whatever workout Taylor has uploaded into the Final Surge app he makes all of us download on the first day of summer conditioning. Most of the team shows up out of fear: the idea of Taylor finding out that you didn't show up to a workout is infinitely more terrifying than the workout itself. Back in the old days, he was well known for smacking the shit out of kids, pinning them up against lockers, spitting in their faces, leaving them to walk home after a bad meet, calling them any variation of faggot that he could land on.

Today is a ten-minute warmup and an 8 *x* 600 alternating between 800 and 400 pace. My bests so far: 5K (cross country)—15:12 on a flat course, 16:08 at Holmdel, 4:18 mile, 9:12 two-mile, 1:57 800, and if I can ride the wave a little longer, some of the D1 coaches that have been in touch should have some slots to throw at me, assuming I can ride the wave a few months longer.

"Forgot my watch," Chase says, hand on my shoulder. "You got the splits?"

"Yeah," I answer, and then we're both off.

2:06, 53.2, 2:05—it's hot but the end of the summer brings in the first few notes of fall and I feel something like a quiet chill in the air as Chase and I round the 300 and close out the first half of the workout.

52.9

"Feel alright?" Chase asks, both of us stretching on the track afterwards. He pours ice down his face and hands me a bottle of Gatorade.

"I'm fine."

"I went out last night. I'm hurting."

"Where?"

"Not really out. Just hid in the basement."

"What were you drinking?"

"Keystone Light."

"Why not just throw your legs behind your head and piss in your own mouth? Seems like it would be roughly the same experience."

"I'll try that next time," he says.

"Did you get drunk?"

"Really drunk."

"You're an idiot."

Chase grabs a bottle of Pedialyte from his bag. My phone vibrates. There's a notification from Instagram—

@mase_314 wants to send you a message.

I am not gone Declan. Come find me.

I freeze. That message, like every personal comment or quote scattered about social media, like everything I've written down inside my story, comes through with the *sound* of Mason's voice: I can hear him saying that, loudly and clearly, inside my own head, and I can hear the voice emanating from the note he left on his bedroom pillow.

"Two minute recovery, Dec. We're . . ." he checks his watch, " . . . about seventy seconds in . . ."

My eyes, still on the phone.

"Dec . . ." a voice from somewhere else. "Dec . . ."

Then I'm back.

"Recovery's for pussies . . . right?" I say, feet on the line. The rest of the team watches curiously. I feel sick, my hands shaking.

"Quit being a try-hard," Carter shouts from afar.

Chase comes up beside me.

"Yeah, yeah," he says. When I lock eyes with Chase, I know he'll follow me. I hit the watch and both of us take off.

I push the 800 hard from the get-go: I'm a hundred in, splitting a 15.5 or so and Chase struggles through the two and the three and at one point I hear him cursing under his breath. Through four, he's still with me, right on me actually, and the 59.3 split is way too hard for what I'm supposed to be doing but I push anyway, through the gentle pain coming through my right ankle at that point, the same pain from the day before that seems to be slowly blossoming into something else. At 600, Chase pulls up alongside and hocks some goo right in front of my line of sight and then he takes off and I chase him through the 700, but in that final straightaway the pain in my ankle gets sharper and he just kicks harder and harder and I can't keep up. He crosses the line about a second or two before I do—the first time in my life that he's gassed me, and only twenty-four hours after I left him behind. I split a 2:02 and he points to his watch: 1:59.9. My ankle, just above the crest of the foot, has gone from a sharp twinge to an actual throbbing pain in tune with my heartbeat.

"What the fuck was that?" Chase says.

I ignore him and rummage through my bag, find my phone, log into Instagram, and check the message again to make sure I hadn't hallucinated it.

"Dec," he says, more quietly.

I fake a smile. "Just wanted to see how that Keystone tastes on the way up."

He shakes his head and says that he isn't gonna puke and then he walks over to the bushes maybe thirty seconds later, puts his fingers in his mouth and pulls the trig.

It's the first time ever that Chase has smoked me, and he makes a point of saying it. I do the rest of the workout with Carter and purposely kick his ass in the final straightaway every time even though the pain starts to get worse and worse,. I hobble away from the final 800 and Chase is the only one who seems to notice.

"Are you alright?" he asks, pointing to my foot, which I haven't stopped rubbing since I started stretching.

"I'm fine."

"You sure?"

"I said I was fine."

Carter and the rest of the guys eventually get in their cars and drive away, and I hear them muttering to themselves as to why they even show up for this shit anyway. Catholic boys are real good at being tough when they're in a car, talking to themselves, well on their way to becoming blossoming Republicans with nine different tabs open in incognito mode.

The sun is almost gone, and Chase stays with me and it's both of us stretching on the track while the moon moves up into the sky and lights us both up.

Later, at a Chipotle, Chase reaches over and eats some of my chips.

"It was definitely better on the way down," he says, my eyes on Instagram and his eyes on me.

That night I stay in and jerk off and try to sleep. There's a party coming up on Friday in Bradley—this time at Carter's house and he makes it a point to say he's having it the day before the long run. It's supposed to be an Eskimos + Hoes themed party. Last month he did a Halfway to Christmas party. Some girl got roofied there last year and they did this whole big cover-up, said she drank too much of the lemonade/Everclear combo they had served in the center of the living room. There's a time warp in these white boy neighborhoods where, if you just close your eyes and imagine somebody baking a rhubarb pie and some hey-honey-I'm-home, gee Pa, it could be 1956. Chase texts to ask if I'm going and I tell him maybe and he says I should, just to see whatever the fuck it's gonna be like.

Chase has been following me around since I was young, hanging on like a puppy. I think I liked him too, maybe something like a best friend, if there ever was that sort of thing. Chase always asked me to stay over when he was a kid, and most times I'd oblige him. Who'd want to fall asleep in his fucking house anyway? Some nights we'd pull up some vanilla porn and jerk off, separate beds and all, pillows placed strategically to keep things out of sight. I remember once Mason catching me with a full spread of naked dudes open on my computer. I whispered a denial so quietly that Mason had to ask me to repeat it and I did, and I was so fucking petrified of his response, but he just put his hand on my head, shuffled my hair.

"Well, at least you won't be as boring as the rest of us."

I think about asking Chase, just talking to him and seeing, but I decide against it and then I'm back on my phone, scrolling through Instagram, staring at the message from the account.

I am not gone, Declan.

I stare for the longest time before punching out a reply.

Who the fuck is this?

The familiar ... pops up and I sit there and wait.

It's me.

That's a lie.

It's your brother.

Fuck off.

Something happened. I want to show you what happened.

You died, Mason. That's what happened.

Do you believe that?

Yes.

I am not gone. I am still here. Come and find me Declan.

Come and find me.

I block the bastard.

3.

I DON'T SLEEP MUCH and when I get to the lot in Asbury the next day, Jake says he's already been there an hour, points to the watch when I walk in.

"You're late," he says.

I check my watch.

"Like two minutes, dude."

Inside he works through the song again and says he's been trying to fill in the gaps, the lyrics that Mason never quite finished, says something about honoring "his vision." He makes up gibberish mostly but then fills in the rest with pictures, boardwalks at night and cigarettes in the rain and all of that, the generalized arsenal from which Mason tended to pull. Slim arrives late, his hair scraggly, his eyes bloodshot and reeking of last night's tequila and body odor. Jake lays into him when he does and when we all finally start rehearsing, Slim drags, like he always does, bass lines walking half a beat behind everything else.

"Slim," Jake says, after we've run through the song two times.

No response, Slim on his phone, diddling away.

"Slim."

"What?"

"Keep up, man."

"Okay."

"Again?"

"Yeah."

"Drop it a beat or three. Just a little."

"Okay."

He slows it down. It's better. He locks eyes with me during the verses. He fills in the first verse with the lyrics that he remembers from Mason and then the second verse he starts to plaster in other stuff. I don't make out the words. I never could with Mason either. It flows nice and smooth. I mostly just ride the hi-hat and keep the snare light and fizzy and the bass drum simple, forceful. We stumble here and there but Jake has a nice voice—real kind of baritone but pretty crisp and clear, and he doesn't fumble over words and even if his lyrical delivery is a little forceful, it never sounds insincere. I think that's the real key with a good singer—you don't need to actually sing well, you just need to sound like you have to sing in order to be well. I never knew much about Jake's story—vanished dad, whispers about his mom being some weird fortune-telling hippie, a brother nobody had ever heard about. Maybe there was more to unpack in him—I wasn't sure.

Later we all sit down and Jake passes me a joint and I take it from his hand and take a few drags. Slim sits a few feet from us, his eyes still on his phone. Jake points to him wordlessly and shakes his head and I look away.

"It's a good song," Jake says.

"Yeah."

"Maybe it's got some legs," he says.

"You know the odds for that? It's a good song. But we'd need luck. We'd need timing. And we'd need money."

"Maybe," he says.

A beat.

"Did he have any others?" he asks quietly.

"What do you mean?"

"Like stuff, you know . . . that he'd showed you. But not me."

"No. I don't know."

"Did he record stuff?"

"On his phone."

"Anything good?"

"I don't know. He recorded a lot."

"But nothing that he showed you."

"Nothing that he showed me."

"I wish he had."

"Why?"

"I don't know. Would've been nice to have more from him. Would've been nice to just have more of him, period."

"Yeah."

He throws the dead joint onto the concrete, strums a few C/A-min ditties on the Strat that he's had slung around his neck the entire time. Slim keeps his eyes locked on his phone, unbothered.

"Alright, let's run it again," Jake says, standing up, smacking his boots onto the ground. I'm with him. Slim takes a few seconds to catch up.

Later that night we're at a house party in Brielle—a gig we've had before at this girl Robin's house that Jake fucked a few times. In the backyard there's a pool and a grill and one of those fire pits with metal and stone sitting in the center of the off-blue veranda, surrounded now by teenagers drinking from Solo cups. The humidity on the air is thick and somebody lights a citronella candle and the smell mixes with the skunked weed that's permeating the air. Some of the kids I recognize but most I don't and as usual the parents are on the porch with frozen margaritas and goblets of Chardonnay and intermingling with the teenagers, cavorting their way back into youth.

When we start the set, everybody's been hammering the tequila grapefruit punch that sits in the center of the party by the pool and so there's some overly enthusiastic *woops* and *woos* when we take the stage and Jake leans into the mic and says we're going to do some cool shit and then he goes into "Back in Black." Jake's vocals are always solid and so he does the best Brian Johnson that he can and for the most part it's a pretty solid start, except the absence of a rhythm guitar is pretty glaring when Jake has to take the solo. Slim doesn't seem to notice, just standing by the stack and grooving along, his bass tone way too treble-y, completely unable to cover up the missing rhythm parts.

Jake takes over for Mase for the rest of the cover songs—slams some ugly, pentatonic solos over Slim's bass. I tell him to turn up the fuzz to mask the emptiness over the lead parts, especially when I move through a crunchy version of "Riders on the Storm" and a too-fast "Man in the Box." Slim drags the whole fucking time. I keep the train rolling, and during "Box" I try to hit the snare drum as hard as I possibly can, especially during the verses, smacking the song along.

"Goddamnit, Slim, keep up," Jake hisses at him before the solo. Slim looks at me and shrugs. "Box" comes and goes, and we move through some other songs and the crowd is noticeably disengaged by the time we're doing "Here Comes Your Man."

Near the end we're supposed to cover "I Wanna Be Sedated" and I'm about to count it off but Jake calls for "Song for the Dead." I hesitate and he calls for it again. He stares at me, locks eyes, nods, and I see him mutter something to himself and look to the sky. He stares at the black for a while before turning back to me and nodding.

Undeterred, Jake slams the first open C.

"This is for my friend," he mutters into the mic.

He takes the first verse by himself, all flanger and chorus and wetness. The song moves nice and slow, and even when he deliberately drags behind the pace, it feels nice. After the first chorus, the band joins in, mostly me with some errant snare hits here and there, working the ride cymbal as gently as I possibly can. He gets to the second chorus and the song really seems to be cruising. All in all, we're improvising the entire time, working through it on stage. Mase's lyrics that Jake doesn't remember he just fills in with words but this time there's some consistency to the syllables, some hint of something, and even if the words are garbled a bit, the melody's there. There's some echo on the Strat and for whatever reason it catches the acoustics of the backyard pretty good and it's almost like the jangle of the guitar is bouncing off the top of the pool. Jake is right: it has that thing—that quality where you've heard it before, you've known it for a thousand years, even if you know it hasn't ever existed. The crowd, initially just as dispassionate as they were through every other song, starts to slow down and congregate around the band, eyes on us, and by the time the final key-change chorus moves in, they are paying careful attention. It's a change of pace, and when Jake brings it down for the final verse, moving slowly again, the song starting to fade away, everyone is relatively quiet: eyes on us, watching this thing germinate before them.

Afterwards, there's applause—not a lot, but more than we're used to, and a lot more than is supposed to come wallowing out of what is normally a Natty Light party for a bunch of half-chubbed douchebags and the poor girls sloughed at their side.

"That was good," Jake mutters off-mic when the song ends and the applause, small as it may be, keeps rolling.

Side of the party and I put my hand on Jake's head and punch Slim in the arm. Jake says he has to find that girl Robin and so he vanishes into the crowd and Slim just stands around looking stupid before I up and ditch him. Out of the crowd some girl comes and puts her hand on my shoulder as I'm walking down the stairs into the basement trying to grab a beer.

"Hell of a song at the end," she says. Nose ring and blond hair and light in her eyes. She is tall and skinny and her skin is tan and she looks profoundly unfamiliar.

"Thanks," I say.

"Was that an original?"

"Yeah."

"Most of the bands that play around here—the originals—just a bag of dicks. That was actually good."

"Thanks," I say again.

"You sticking around?" she asks.

"I don't know. Probably not."

"You want to stick around?"

I look around the basement. A couple of kids making out on the couch, boys and girls. Jake and Slim nowhere to be seen. I shake my head.

"Not really," I say. "Nothing to do with you."

"Harsh," she says, handing me a flip phone.

"A flip phone."

"Works like any other. Put your number in," she says.

"Come on," I laugh. "Nobody has these anymore."

"They still had keypads in the Stone Age. Put your number in."

I eye her for a second and then plug in the digits, hand her the phone back.

"Elizabeth. Lizzy preferably," she says, hand out. I shake it.

"Declan," I say. "Preferably."

"Well, I will see you around." She turns away, heading up the stairs, moving past a body and another body before vanishing. I wait for a while for her to reappear. She doesn't. I find the beer fridge and pull out a Keystone and open it and watch the kids making out for a while before taking a few sips and then I'm bored so I leave.

In the car, I'm rereading the new Mason account's messages and watching videos of dead Mason surfing from last summer on his real account. He catches a couple of the waves and then there's a run where he keeps falling down. I watch the video over and over. I can't remember where or why I took it. I scroll through the suggested videos. The algorithm vomiting dead kid cancer stories, beheadings, jorkin memes, and a recipe for barbacoa tacos. I'm back on the new account. I tell myself that my brother is dead, but I can't pull myself away from the words inside my inbox. I block it again.

Chase texts me, gives me a reason to leave. I ask him if he wants to get drunk cause I can't think of anything else to do. He says that we've got practice tomorrow but I ask him again and tell him that it'll just be us two drinking and he says yeah, sounds good, where at?

We're at the track, drinking from a bottle of icy Jack Daniels that Chase keeps in a Yeti. There's a moon hanging over the track half-crescent and lighting up the night. The chittering around—the bugs and the crickets and the cicadas, every once in a while the whoosh of a bat moving through the night.

"Met a girl," I say, fingering the bottle of Jack.

"Yeah?"

"At the show."

"Hot?"

"Yeah. I guess."

"Do anything?"

"Met her for like thirty seconds."

"Should've fucked her. You wouldn't have needed more than thirty seconds anyway."

I nod, smiling.

"Didn't seem like an option at the time." I point to the booze.

"Oh well," he says.

"My brother's been texting me," I say.

"What?" he says, squinting.

"Some fucked up account. Says it's him."

"That's fucked," he says.

"Yeah, it's weird. It's—it also . . . he's saying the stuff that Mason said the night he died. It's really weird."

"Probably some stupid fuck just dicking around. Like Timmy."

A beat.

"Sorry," he says, "if you were thinking it was like . . . actually him."

"No, I wasn't, but like . . . kind of. I don't know. It would be nice."

I gesture toward the bottle.

"This stuff. Christ, man. This sucks," I say.

"I don't know. Better than most of the shit we drink."

"Remember last summer at Casey's?"

"Yeah."

"Fucking disgusting, man."

"Banker's."

"I don't think . . . I don't know. I don't think there's anybody on Earth who takes shots of vodka. Except us."

"I guess you have to learn somehow," I say.

"What was your first drink?"

"Like ever?"

"Yeah."

"I don't know. I think my mom let us have beer at a Halloween party once. I think we were in like fifth grade."

"A full beer."

"Like a shot of beer."

"Ah."

"You?"

"Last summer."

"The vodka shots?"

"Yeah."

"Jesus Christ, man. That's how you started drinking? You never told me that."

"Didn't seem relevant."

"Fucking shots, man."

"I hate shots. Always fucks up my dick," he says.

"Like you have any dick to fuck up."

He tilts the bottle upside down with his fingers on top of it, turns it right side up, flicks a speck of whiskey at me.

"Fuck you," he says, smiling.

A beat.

"What's the weirdest shit you've ever jerked off to?" he says.

"Jesus Christ, dude. Chill."

"What? I'm just asking. Everybody does it."

"'Everybody does it.' You sound like fucking Mr. Carpenter."

"No if I sounded like Mr. Carpenter, I'd be two feet behind you and whispering in your ear."

"I guess," I say.

"With the nicotine breath and the wispy ear hair."

"Plenty of ear hair," I say.

A beat.

"So what's the answer?" he says.

"I don't know. Nothing too weird. You?"

"Same."

We both get drunker. Time passes.

"This girl Kara is trying to fuck me," Chase says.

"From Point?"

"Yeah."

"Isn't she the one with the missing toe?"

"Yeah," he says, nodding. "Yeah."

"At least she has a fun party trick."

"Fuck you," Chase says.

"She's hot though," I say.

"Yeah. Pretty hot."

"What are you waiting for?"

"Not my type," he offers.

"That girl tonight seemed cool," I say.

"Yeah?" he says.

"Yeah."

"Cool how?"

"I don't know. A little weird."

"Most girls are," he says.

"Yeah," I say. "She was weird in a cool way. Like alternative chick."

"Emo-chick."

"Not emo. Cool. Off the beaten path. That kind of thing."

The conversation goes silent and all both of us can hear are the cicadas and crickets and the occasional grind of tires bleating down the main road. At one point I think I hear him turning his head to me like he has something to say, but he doesn't say it and I turn to face the street and listen to the engines in the distance and the bugs and the swish of the bats in the air. At some point, he brings up Carter and we rag on him together, shrimp-dicked Nazi douchebag, and everything feels fine again but the breaths and the pauses and the quiet all seem full and waiting.

When I'm drunk enough, I bet Chase that he can't beat me in a 400, and he halfheartedly agrees. I toe up on the line again, take my shirt off, and try to get some semblance of balance back. Mosquitoes start laying into me and he's got his shirt off too and we're both just wearing board shorts, so the run itself is going to be stupid to begin with. But we line up again, sandals now off, and he lines up with me, just like he's done forever, and it feels something like comfort. I hit the watch and go.

I move out hard and he follows but pretty quickly it slows down and everything seems to go still and move in syncopation. Piss-drunk at midnight and trying to throw down as we round the first 100 and I feel the booze in my stomach churning and some kind of impending headache already starting its journey upwards. People talk about the magical bullshit of running: the healing power of athletics. Fuck that—I just always liked beating people, winning. At some point we're shoulder to shoulder, moving at the same pace, not even bothering to fake a challenge.

And then our bodies remember that we're both toasted and when the final move from 300 to 400 is torture and it's worse torture when we come to a full stop and all the booze starts shifting upward from stomach to esophagus to the back of your throat till we're spewing yellow and orange into the bushes.

"Fuck," he whispers.

"Big mistake," I say. "Sorry."

"No need to apologize."

We puke a little more and a lot more and a little more. Eventually it's just back to the quiet again and Chase sits down in the grass and crosses his legs, facing me.

"Do you miss him?" he asks, thin filaments of yellow goo hanging from his lips.

"You asked me that before," I say, wiping my mouth and joining him on the grass.

"I don't know what to say about it. You can talk to me if you want. I don't know. I'm drunk."

"He was bad at the end. He was . . . all over the place. He'd always been wild. His brain and stuff. Just couldn't focus on one thing. Always consumed by the world and shit. But at the end he just . . . stopped. It wasn't like he had an episode or some freakout or something. He just stopped . . . *being*. Like he was being erased from the page."

"Like he didn't even know who he was anymore," Chase says.

"Yeah. Kind of like that."

"Do you ever feel that way?"

"Which way?"

"Confused. About yourself. Do you . . . I don't know what I'm asking. Like you're living in somebody else's skin."

"We're whoever we say we are, I think, until we aren't. Mason pretended to be this hip, attuned, alternative rock-and-roll badass. Convinced a lot of people. He even convinced me. Turns out he was just a coward."

A pause.

"Sorry," I say.

"It's fine."

"I'm just . . . "

"It's okay."

A beat.

"Hear anything about his body yet?"

"No."

"That sucks," he says sheepishly.

"You want to stay over or what?"

We're home at midnight, drunk. We rummage through the kitchen. We spill glasses of water and we fumble for more liquor. I stare at the front door and wait for Mason to walk in, to tell me he's just been out for a bit, that he's coming home again, but the door stays shut. The door is always shut.

We're on the couch and we keep drinking. We turn on the TV and stare at the headlines. The news runs the latest story: more violence and more whispers of violence come to life. The woman on the TV says the video to come is graphic and that they're warning viewers and whatnot. They mention something about homegrown terror, a rising tide of weirdo nationalist groups spreading beneath the surface.

On the video, whoever they are, they corral random local officials in random towns in random locales across the country and videotape them in various dimly lit rooms, gags tied through their mouths. There's a montage cut of several different rooms, several different people, all tied up the same way, all roughly the same distance from the camera. A voice off-screen makes them read the kind of statements you'd hear read in Third World countries—vindication of the mind and the march towards the promised land and taking back the country from the evil inside itself. The video on the screen is a man and a woman, both of them nearly choked with the rope in their mouth, both of them with sweat stains down the center of their shirts, both of their chests heaving, terrified. I watch the faces of the hostages tremble, eyes wet and frightened and hair disheveled. Then there's a tub of gasoline and a match, a flash of light. There's no screaming, just squirming, bodies writhing and twisting and collapsing onto the ground.

Before bed we find some sparklers in the garage and we go out back and light them in the dark and just sort of stand there with the fire crackling in front of us.

I find a pack of Mason's cigarettes inside the toolboxes in the garage and we smoke the entire pack, run through each cigarette with more and more demented purpose. We don't really even take any good pulls—just mow each dart down wordlessly. Everything spins and my mouth is chalk dry.

Upstairs we both watch some porn and click through progressively more depraved things and pretend to be interested but we just shut the computer after some weird gangbang thing and go to sleep.

※

The next night, Taylor stands over Chase and I and watches us both puking into the dirt. He calls today's practice at the Manasquan Reservoir instead of the park and I barely make it two miles into the five-mile loop before I start retching—it's been almost 24 hours since we both started drinking but I forgot to hydrate along the way and the morning we both spent at the beach eating pork rolls and trying to sweat out the alcohol, and the Pedialyte/water combo that we've been housing all afternoon hasn't worked for either of us, and the loops at Manasquan are way more of a bitch than the ones at Thompson—a five-mile doozy that has about four different runs inside of it, hills and straightaways and woods and steady climbs—a fucking ball-breaker sober, a death kiss hungover. Vomiting comes so easily that it almost distracts me from the searing pain in my ankle that I've been ignoring. The kicker is that the run itself isn't even that hard: the workout was supposed to be an easy ten minutes, a forty-minute progression, and another easy ten. I make it about fourteen minutes into the progression before I start spitting up bile and once Chase sees the first gag he follows suit. The rest of the team leaves us at the two-mile marker and continues the loop.

Taylor hovers over both of us, yellow bile dripping out from our mouths.

"It was my idea," I say.

Chase catches my eye.

"No. I made him do it," he says.

After a second, Taylor leaves us both to puke and tells us to meet at the start of the loop, says that maybe the walk will do some good. When we make it there, the team has finished the first loop and the silence that comes when we both show up means they already know what's coming.

Taylor kicks both of us off the team but makes us stay to watch the rest of the guys finish the workout. The rest of them crush it, especially Carter, who seems to be running with some newfound purpose. Taylor calls the squad over and points at both of us. Then he stares at us for the longest time. He doesn't say anything but everything is clear and so, together, Chase and I leave.

In the car, Chase driving—I'm staring at the @mase_314 account—the inbox, waiting to be filled.

4.

CHASE LIVES IN SHARK RIVER, maybe five minutes from my house so I follow him there and both of us sit outside on his porch sweating and I make it a point when he jumps in the pool to check my phone again, out of compulsion, desire, not sure. I go to the dead account and unblock the username, but there's no messages from Mason, The Ghost, whoever has been texting me. Chase stretches for a while and one of his balls drops out of his running shorts as he's rolling out his quads and he puts it away when he catches me staring. The sun's setting and my iPhone flashes notifications about possible suicide bombings in California and a hybrid disease built in a lab being spread in the drinking water somewhere near Tallahassee, rumors about homegrown terrorism. When I check Instagram, the account is still there: @mase_0314.

"Mom, what does this mean?" I'd asked, and when Mom took a look at the note, she pushed me aside and snatched her cell phone from the kitchen countertop

In the hallway in the middle of the night after he died: rapping my fingers on the walls and waiting for a rapping to come echoing back.

Chase comes out of the pool and I look away and he tells me that he thinks Taylor will text us later and all will be forgiven—he can't win without us and he knows it. Chase pulls up next to me, real close, and shows me an old Snap story of Taylor drunkenly rambling on about winning a national title and the legacy of the program and then Chase just shows me random videos he likes, a golden retriever trying to put a calico kitten to sleep or a wounded swan reunited with its partner. His dad is behind both of us but neither of us notice until the swan video is over and I watch him tap the pool chair and tap my shoulder and ignore Chase.

"Hey. . . ." Chase says, peering behind him cautiously.

His dad just taps his fingers over and over and walks down the patio, opens a beer from the mini-fridge outside, and falls down on one of the recliners, sunglasses on.

Thunderstorms roll in and I leave Chase's house and he tells me we'll meet up tomorrow to run. When I get home, I head upstairs and open Instagram.

Tell me things about Mason.
If you're really him. Tell me.

I sit and wait for a reply but nothing comes and I refresh the homepage for the account that sits still blank and then I get bored.

It's ten at night and I'm on the couch when I hear Mom come in. I keep my eyes glued to the TV set and I hear her shuffling behind me.

"Where were you?" I ask.

"I was out."

"Where?"

"To the college. Walked around. I saw that girl Abigail from the seminar last spring—on campus early I guess. Kids go back earlier and earlier these days."

Mom walks over to the fridge and opens it, pulls out a bottle of white wine with one of those stoppers in it.

"That bored?" I ask.

"Not bored, Declan," she says, grabbing a stemless wine glass from the cabinet and hurriedly dumping the remainder of the bottle inside. "Bored would be a privilege."

"When do classes start up?"

"Two weeks."

"Okay."

"But they offered me a sabbatical."

"And?"

She shrugs.

"I'm taking it. I think. I don't know."

"Take it. What time are your classes supposed to be this year?"

"Seven to ten. Monday, Tuesday, Thursday. Three-three. All of them."

"Take the sabbatical."

"It's a good way to vent grief," she says. "Teaching, that is."

"So is smoking weed on the couch."

"I beg to differ, Declan."

"Just take the sabbatical. Fuck the school."

"Language."

"Fuck the school. Take some time. Sigmund Freud will be there when you come back."

"Horned up as ever," she says.

"Fucking-A, Mom. Gross."

"Language."

She watches as I'm staring at the wine glass in her hand.

"Five stages of grief," she says.

"Which one is this?"

"I'm bargaining today," she says.

"Well, I didn't say anything."

"I know, but I can see your eyes."

"I didn't say anything."

She takes a long sip.

"I want a cigarette," she says. "I would kill for a cigarette."

"I mean—" I start. "Mason had a bunch upstairs."

"He did?"

"Yeah."

"Where?"

We're upstairs now, in my room. I reach behind my nightstand and pull out a pack of Marlboros.

"He made me hide them," I say. "He figured you'd never imagine me smoking."

"Yeah, well he was right," she says, taking the pack out of my hands. She takes a long gaze around the room, at the music posters and the running shoes and some of the trophies I've won and the computer sitting open on the desk.

"How's the story?" she asks, pointing to the computer. She's staring at the wall now, glasses on the bridge of her nose. She smells like the perfume she wore to Mason's funeral, cigarettes.

"It's still bullshit."

She pulls out one of the cigarettes, looks around.

"Here," I say, fumbling inside of my desk drawer. I pull out a pack of matches and hand her one. She strikes the match on the edge of the desk and lights the cigarette, blows smoke in the room. With the light behind her she looks smaller, more diminished. She was never light but never too thin and now she looks like the skin on her face is retreating, moving back inside of her, and the eyes inside of her head shrinking, the hair on her head thinning, the blood in her veins growing bluer and more crystalline, the life inside of her depleting. I imagine her swinging her legs out of bed in the morning, for what exactly, I don't know.

"I haven't replaced the smoke alarms upstairs in years," she says, brushing her hair back and taking another drag.

There's a moment of quiet and we're staring around the room, waiting for the person next door to walk in.

"I don't know what else to do with all of it," I say.

"Every time I think it's getting manageable it catches on something, a memory or a flash or his face, and the wound is torn open again." She looks at me, red eyes. "It hurts worse than I could ever have imagined anything could hurt."

A beat.

"We're doing okay, Ma."

"Yeah, how?"

"Cause we're still moving."

She tosses me a quasi-smile, gestures for me to follow her.

Downstairs she offers a slice of cold pizza from the fridge. I take it. I move into the chair next to her and just put her head on my shoulder and sit there and she says that it's her fault and she should've known and she's the adult in the room and she should've seen something and how could she have missed the signs and then she says that Mason's heart was a thousand times larger than hers and she never knew how to deal with it, all of his heart and his love and his hate, and she says that if she could stretch her hand through time to that night she would run her hands through his hair and hold him tight the moment he walked out the door and tell him that she doesn't remember life before her first seconds with him and that existence itself began with him.

Mom wandering in circles in the kitchen, his note in one hand and her cell in the other hand: "Jesus Christ, Mase, please pick up the phone. Pick up the goddamn phone. . . ."

I lean into Mom harder, the glass of wine in her hand, her breath full of alcohol and cigarettes and for some reason it feels like something warm and comforting. The dark comes again though, quickly—and I feel like it may come like this forever, each moment of peace and silence and reverie undercut with the dark.

"I'm going to bed Mom," I say.

"You want to watch some videos?" she says.

"No. Not really."

She smiles sadly. "Okay."

"I can help you pick out some shoes if you were serious."

She doesn't turn, eyes on the TV. "I'd like that," she offers.

When I go upstairs I wait about ten minutes and listen and sure enough, I hear the static and the familiar sound of Mason's prepubescent voice coming through the speakers, and it feels like this is a memory I can actually picture, so I sneak downstairs and watch from just outside the kitchen, my eyes deep into the living room and Mason's ghost on the television, my mom holding a glass of whiskey in her hand—

A lake cabin that the family rented in the Poconos, both me and my brother trying to learn how to waterski and Dad willfully dragging the boys again and again until we figured it out. The weather was overcast and cloudy and humid and Dad insisted on life jackets and Mom insisted on taking every picture or video she could. Mason was a short, chubby kid when he was younger, before he stretched out. He's standing at the edge of the dock, watching me out on the water try to stand every time Dad took the boat around for another spin. Every time I fall he laughs and every time I stand up he gets quiet and points and makes sure that Mom is watching.

"Took him long enough," he says after the first time I'm up for more than a second or two, his voice a pitched siren.

"Relax, Mase. Be good," she says, her voice floating from behind the camera.

"It took him thirty minutes, Mom."

"You're his brother. You can show him the way. You can show him the good or the bad, the ups and the downs. Just remember that."

"Okay," Mase says quietly.

I watch myself come in from the water. Dad comes into the frame, built like a linebacker and decked out in a bad Hawaiian shirt and out-of-place cargo shorts and carrying a koozie with a Bud Light at the center of it. I have my head down and I remember feeling embarrassed.

"It was good, Dec. You did good," Mase says. I remember the embarrassment lifting into the clouds.

That night I check the account again—no reply.

I can't sleep so I walk around the hallways upstairs, wood floors creaking beneath me. Mason's room stands closed, a tomb, and I stand outside it for a second, listening to all of the nothing, the smell of Mom's cigarettes still on the air.

Carter texts and asks if we're still on the team and even if we're not whether he can steal a few handles from Mom's cabinet and I think about buying a voodoo doll with his name on it and violating it with a mechanical pencil. I send a message to Chase and ask him when and where we're meeting for the run—he says around five or so with the start at his house. Today's run is an OYO and it's supposed to be done on some kind of flat surface—a buildup for fifty minutes that ends with about five minutes of an all-out blitz. I like buildups—the start is easy and it gets funky in the middle but if I can survive to the end the adrenaline always kicks in and the last five minutes feel like lightning. Chase has more natural speed than I do but he doesn't do quite as well with any kind of aerobic endurance, so he usually needs me in the beginning of the race and less so at the end. It's why during the season he struggles in races where somebody takes it out hard—if he can hang at a slower pace for 2K or so, he's got a better kick at the end than anybody in the state. If somebody takes it out harder than he's comfortable with, he has trouble surviving. So we need each other for these kinds of buildups. I start to stretch on the floor and when I put pressure down on one spot in my ankle the pain lights up my whole right leg. The thunderstorms from the night before don't break the humidity—they just seem to make it worse, and even around five, it's still fucking miserable.

The air is heavy and wet and gross and even breathing is difficult.

I meet Chase outside his house and I point to a bruise on his arm and he says he fell out of bed the night before. I've loaded up on Advil but the ankle still hurts.

"You sure?" I ask, losing the shirt and watching Chase lose his.

"Dude, it's just a bruise," he says.

The plan is to cut down to the boardwalk and take it into Spring Lake and cut back at the halfway point. It's about two miles from Chase's to the start of the boards and that first mile is pretty slow: 7:15 or so. A few times I try to push it a little harder, but Chase doesn't follow and my ankle is already hurting enough. When I hit the boards, I pick up the pace as slowly as I can, and when we cross under the Belmar arches into Spring Lake, the Garmin on my wrist tells me we've dropped to 6:45 which is still slow but moving in the right direction. The sweat starts to come off both of us and we notice other walkers and joggers, women carting babies and overweight dudes in sweat-soaked Nike apparel, dodging out of our way as we start barreling towards the pavilion. We push the pace harder despite the pain—fuck it. Chase follows but I hear his breath getting more and more ragged.

"Let's roll," I say, faking ease.

As my heart rate climbs and climbs, I let my mind wander—all the things I've thought about Chase and all the things I imagine he's thought about me. Maybe I'm wrong and I'm making it up. I wanna drop him again—get away from whatever's pummeling through my mind at this point. Maybe he'll stay with me no matter how hard I push it. I check my watch: 6:05 and just under three miles and the pain is moving beyond that familiar throb into something worse, sharp stabs on each step, but I'm a goddamn idiot so I keep rolling anyway, and I imagine myself as the hero of my own narrative and Rocky never fucking gave up so here we go: we're not halfway done with the run and I know I'm already ahead of what I know Chase can handle but I don't want to drop or bail or look like a pussy. I keep moving anyway. It always came naturally: running was like flying, and for Chase, it was just something else he had to prove to himself, his dad, whatever. Chase's dad was the kind of one-dimensional human that gets eaten by the titular monster in the most horrible way, usually after throwing a puppy into its jaws or something.

"Stop pushing the pace," Chase says, each word cut off by a sharper intake of breath.

"You can do it. Stay with me," I say.

I'm aware that this run is going to fucking break me, but at least I can drag Chase ahead of me before it does.

"Stay with me," I repeat.

"I can't."

"Yeah you can, man. Yeah you can."

"Fuck."

"Stay with me, Chase. Stay with me."

Somehow he does, and by the time we've reached the halfway point (about four miles in), I can tell that he's dragging but, bless his fucking heart, he's keeping with it, and his breathing, scattered and asthmatic at the start, settles into something of a rhythm. I stop and reverse the course to head home, and our pace is hovering around 5:50, faster than we're supposed to be moving. The skies start to open up and most of the people clear from the boardwalk but both of us stay, rain barreling down and waves crashing in the distance and lightning exploding over the barely visible buildings in Asbury miles and miles up the coast.

I dropped Chase only a few days ago but something keeps him with me the entire run, past the second pavilion and past the giant Essex Hotel on Ocean Avenue and past snack bars and bikers fleeing from the rain, past grandmothers and grandfathers abandoning daily walks, past the feeling I get now every time it rains, and I'm lucky that the rain is hard enough that Chase can't see me cry, and I imagine my brother standing up in the sky and pulling open the clouds the way he used to rip open the curtains in the morning if I wasn't awake when he needed me to be—the knives slicing down, up and down my leg, at this point don't have a fucking thing on that feeling of wanting so badly to be woken up early, to have cold water splashed on me while I'm showering, to be called a fucking pussy one minute and the best brother he could've had the next. I push the pace even harder and now it's something close to an all-out sprint, about ten minutes before the run's supposed to end and I just want to hurt as badly as I can, to feel the entire inside of that leg crush and cave and chew and tear and rip and break and splinter into a thousand fucking pieces and snap tendons so hard they break skin and compound fracture tibias and fibias and compress capillaries into grape jelly. At one point, I let out a fucking scream. Chase does the same.

But he hangs on the entire time.

4:44 for the last leg.

We finish about a quarter mile from Chase's house and the rain is pouring down—we can barely see one another, and the first step I take is an absolutely fucking agonizing hobble. Chase notices.

"You're hurt, dude," he shouts through the rain.

"You kept up," I say, ignoring him, tears pouring out.

"You took it too hard. You're hurt." Chase puts his hand on my head and pushes. I push back. Then he puts his hand back on my head, and we both just sort of stand there, staring at each other. I watch as he brushes the rain out of his eyes and for a second I'm ashamed.

"You kept up, Chase. You're better than you think."

He watches through the rain and doesn't speak, and when he does, it's hardly a whisper.

"Let's get the fuck out of here."

The rain keeps coming and coming and when we make it to Chase's house nobody's home.

ᛯ

Inside the pitter-patter on the roof picks up and I listen to the beat of it as it hammers the house. Chase brings me upstairs and says he has some clothes to change into if I want and that he needs to shower and that he's going first because I was the dickhead who made him run that hard.

"You should see a doctor," he says.

"Maybe," I mutter.

He wraps the towel around his waist and shucks the shorts onto the floor underneath the towel.

"I'll be in the shower," he says.

"Okay," I say, eyes down.

"You gotta see a doctor about that. I'm serious."

I nod.

"I'm gonna shower," he repeats.

I stand there shivering and I wait for him to respond and then he goes into the bathroom and leaves the door open an inch or two. I wrap my arms around myself and the rain gets louder and louder and I can feel my heart beating inside my throat. For a moment I just watch the steam start to exit the tiny crack in the door and then he opens the door without anything on.

"Are you coming in or what?"

So I follow him in and once the shower door shuts he turns and faces me.

"Dude what are we—"

Ӿ

When we both come out the shame is gone so there's no towel on either of us, and then a voice cuts through the moment.

"What is this?"

Chase's dad enters the room, takes a quick, nonchalant look at both of us, shrugs.

He winds up and cracks Chase across the face with the back of his hand and Chase just sails across the hallway and lands on his back completely naked and I hear his head crack against the hardwood with a wet smack. At first, there's no expression of surprise on Chase's face and he doesn't protest and his dad calls him a faggot under his breath and then his dad is kneeling on the ground, pinning Chase's throat to the carpet with his left knee and smashing his face in again and again with his right fist. He winds up more quickly each time and Chase at some point just stops trying to defend himself with his hands that are wet with water and wet with fresh blood and just lays there taking it and whimpering until one punch cracks his nose and a near-arterial spray of blood squirts out and over his chest and some of it gets on my foot and then he's just crying loudly and terrible and now a river of blood streaming down his face and then I hear his mom coming up the stairs screaming and I've watched the entire thing without moving before his dad just turns and stares at my naked frame and I take a step like I'm going to hit him or kill him or do anything but then he moves to me and says to get the fuck out of here and that all faggots get the same treatment and he tells his wife to get downstairs and make herself useful by grabbing some fucking towels and I grab my shorts from the floor and almost slip on the blood sprinting as I stumble down the hardwood stairs and out the front door and I feel like such a fucking coward as I hear Chase start screaming again and the sound of another hit and another and another and another and even as my ankle throbs and the pain like a knife shoots up my leg with each step, I start to run.

When I walk in the door the rain has all but stopped but I'm soaking wet and Mom happens to be standing in the hallway with a glass of brown liquor in her hand when I walk in, the same ridiculous blue flowing robe on her. She takes one look and her face drops and she comes over saying my name over and over again and she grabs my hands and holds them out and for the first time I see the blood all down my chest and arms that the rain hasn't washed away.

"It's not mine I promise. Mom it's not mine," but she grabs me hard and pulls me in and I keep repeating that I'm okay, but she just cries and says my name over and over.

"Mom it's fine. It's not mine."

I say it again. She just says my name.

"Mom," I say, and then I say it again, my head in her shoulder, and then I am burying myself inside of her shoulder. We just stand in that hallway for what feels like forever talking at each other until our voices get quieter and quieter and it's just the sound of the rain starting up again.

Upstairs I take another shower and clean off the blood and then I wait for the text from Chase but it doesn't come, so I scroll through Snap stories and Twitter and Instagram and try to block it all out. Twitter reminds me that there's a congressional election coming up and that the fate of the country rests on it or something like that. I scroll through Carter's stories—mostly just liquor and Milwaukee's Best he's hoarding for the party tomorrow with bad captions (a picture of Stoli and an Eskimo hat—*"chilled to perfection"*). I think about calling the police on Chase's dad, but I picture the scene after the police leave and all the nightmares that it would bring and I can't bring myself to make the call.

I walk down the hallway to Mason's room: the forbidden tomb, think about going inside. I stand there for a while and nothing happens.

In my room, I open @mase_0314.

Can you pretend?

I send the message over to the account and wait.

The dot-dot-dot lights up again.

Pretend what?

To be him. To be my brother.

Just typing the message feels noxious and awful but Mason's room is empty and the clothes on the floor will stay on that floor until somebody moves them and that secret would stay under that floorboard until the house rotted away—just a snapshot of the rest of the world moving forward without him, like all of it never mattered in the first place, like he was never part of any plan, like everything just counts for nothing.

Wherever you got your info—use it.

There's no game.

I don't believe you.

Believe. I am not gone.

I know the person on the other end is a fake, but I still imagine Mason peering down from the sky and reaching his hand out but never quite getting there. For even just a second nothing seems like it can shatter the illusion that I'm talking to him through my phone like he was just away for a while at a concert up north, at a school trip that Mom forced him to go on, even just at the beach down the road smoking weed and watching dolphins float out not 500 yards from the shore, or even just dead, but not dead in the way that we know it, dead in a different way, dead in the way we've always wanted people to die: just a temporary exit, a delayed reunion, a promise that there would be another day, somewhere, after it all went black.

So I pretend. Every message that comes through that phone comes through in Mason's voice, still alive, and I don't stop and I don't want to stop until I can hear him in my head.

I want another chance.

Another chance at what?

At that night. The night you died.

You'll see me again soon.

I could've said something. I could've asked you to stay in and watch a movie. I could've ordered a fucking pizza. Anything. And if I can't have that, I want that moment. I want that final convo. That's all I want—you could go and die again if I just could talk to you one more time. Ask you questions. Get answers before you left. That's what you left us with, Mase: questions and more questions. Why?

The dot-dot-dot lights up again and vanishes. I wait and wait but nothing comes. Chase texts me and says he's coming over.

You there? I ask Mason.

Mason, you there?

Mason?

Downstairs, Mom picks at one of those unfrozen Trader Joe's meals, hand on another stemless glass of Chardonnay or Sauvignon Blanc or whatever-the-fuck, not speaking, but when Chase walks in the door, she wakes up in a way I haven't seen since before Mase.

"Oh, honey."

In what must be seconds she's got a dish towel with ice wrapped inside of it on his nose and mouth, and she spots the blood over his body and she looks at me another time and her expression shifts to something like understanding. I don't say anything, but I put my head down and Chase does the same. She makes us both come inside and sit but she doesn't make either of us talk or explain ourselves. All three of us just sit in the kitchen and listen to the rain come down tirelessly outside.

"Is it ever gonna stop?" he asks, trying to break the silence.

"The rain?" I say.

"Yeah," he says, looking around, his hand holding the bloodied, soaked towel up to his face.

"I don't know."

"It'll stop. It always does," Mom says quietly, her eyes on both of us.

Chase's eyes are red. Mom looks at me seriously.

"Well let's go, both of you. Come on."

Chase and I sit in the backseat and Mom says to make sure that he holds the ice pack with enough pressure. On the car ride there, all three of us hatch a story—a fight at the boardwalk with a benny that went awry—we even give him the name Vinny to add some authenticity. She never asks what really happened but I imagine she's pieced it together—the way she used to piece together a bad day at school based on a fleeting expression or the way I'd walked in the front door: the disadvantages of an overly analytical professor as a mother. Chase thanks her and at one point in the dark he reaches for my hand and wraps his fingers around mine and I want to pull back but I don't.

ᛉ

At the hospital, when Chase is already being checked out, I ask Mom if she wants to know what really happened but she says she already has a guess.

"Mom. . . ."

"You can say the words if you want."

"I don't know. It's not like that."

"It's okay if you are."

"Please can we just not talk about it?"

She shakes her head and smiles. "I'm your mother."

"I don't know, Mom. I really don't."

They set Chase's nose and clean up some of the scrapes and scratches and tell him that a dentist will have to fix up his mouth. The doctor buys the story, even the Vinny part.

That night I'm in bed falling asleep with the account in front of me.

Please come back.

Please.

I watch the dot-dot-dot light up and then vanish. I wait for it to come back. It doesn't. I try to stay awake. There's no answer.

5.

Friday's run is a forty-minute tempo. I lace up and walk out the door and start. I don't get more than ten steps in before the pain comes shooting back. After I scroll through Google until I find a doctor who'll take me that day, some dude with a long Jewish name in Marlboro.

Later, that old man with the Doc Brown look puts his fingers up and down my right ankle and shins and when he presses on a certain place I shoot up from the chair in pain. He orders an X-ray just down the hall and an hour later I'm back in his office with his left fingers still on the same spot, but his right pointed at the black and white scroll of bones up on the board.

"You see that line there? That's a stress fracture. Pretty bad one too. You said you'd felt this for a bit?"

"Just a few days."

"Did you stop when it hurt?"

Ha. Ha. Ha.

"Sorry you hit some bad luck, kid."

I ask about the season. I know the answer before he offers it.

Timmy Carter's party comes that night. Chase texts but I don't even know what to feel at this point. I wander around the party with the new boot and explain to almost everybody what happened. When I tell Carter he laughs and I think about driving my fist through his face. This girl Kara comes up, black hair and nose ring and a Tom Petty shirt and the smell of cigarettes on her tongue and she's drunk so she says she gives good blowjobs. I shrug and she takes me upstairs and gives me one. I stare at the ceiling fan the entire time, and afterwards she asks me if I'm from around here and I tell her I just want to stay quiet.

Later she tries to talk to me in the stairwell and I give her a couple of the briefest answers I can and then she gets the hint and vanishes and I text Lizzy from the show and ask her if she wants to go somewhere sometime, anywhere. I'm standing around the liquor in the kitchen and pretending to pay attention to whatever's being discussed, and eventually the group all just disperses with one another to quiet rooms upstairs. I stay in the basement the rest of the night, listen to the shit EDM coming out of the speakers, watch some of the nerdier crew who somehow made it in the door (likely through the acquisition of liquor) run through Kirby's Island on *Super Smash Bros.* I keep checking my phone and waiting for a text but it never comes.

The night goes on and the party gets quieter and quieter and it all gets a little less cool, becomes more and more like scenes out of awkward memories from eighth-grade basements drinking So-Co out of an antique coffee mug, the splash of pong cups or a beer can hitting the floor intermingled with the sounds of laughter and creaking floorboards coming from upstairs. I step outside at one point, and Timmy's parents are just standing on the porch, passing a joint between each other, unbothered by the surrounding proceedings.

Lizzy answers before I even call the Uber: *name the time*

Outside I sit and wait for the Uber and when I get home, I see Mom standing in the kitchen staring out the window. The rain comes again just as I leave the car, and I stand there in the rain. The rain doesn't stop. Mom watches the entire time and when I smile, she smiles back.

The day of the long run comes and I haven't texted Chase back—I know he does most of the long runs on the boards so I go down and sit at the Playa Bowls and wait for him to pass. He doesn't show, so I toss out the half-eaten açai bowl and leave.

At home, Mom's cleaning the kitchen and throwing away stacks of leftover mail and bills and even some of the newspaper articles she'd saved after he died.

I grab a giant serving bowl and the entire box of Captain Crunch that's been sitting there since, and pour most of it into the bowl, add some milk.

"You'll be back at it someday," she says.

I'm holding the phone in my hand, staring at the inbox of DMs and waiting. I go into the suggested pages and scroll through more dead things and car crash videos and then back to the DMs and back to the car crash videos and I just keep doing this ad nauseum while the TV sounds like a siren in front of me.

She pauses.

"I'm gonna get drunk," she says.

She goes to the liquor cabinet and pulls out a bottle of tequila and triple sec. She moves to the cabinet, finds a shaker, grabs some ice from the freezer, and fills the shaker with all of it. Then she's shaking it up and down, pouring it into a plastic cup and topping it off with some lime juice from the fridge. She stirs it around and takes a sip.

"Brutal," she says.

She grabs the trash bag and pulls it up and closed. "One step at a time," she says, already halfway out the room.

I house the bowl of cereal and then just sit and wallow in the lactose bloating, turn on the television. A children's hospital blown up in the South. A group of domestic terrorists hiding in sleeper cells in the woods of Pennsylvania. A congressman who fucked his own daughter on camera. They say that the hospital and the sleeper cells have a name, and they call them The Liberators.

Mom gets sloshed throughout the day, keeps filling and refilling her margarita glass, putting on alt-rock songs that get weirder and weirder, diving more and more into the pack of Marlboros that is nearly empty by the time she's on her fourth cup of booze that by this point is mostly just tequila and melted ice. She throws away trash and old mail and whatever else. She doesn't speak much, just wanders around the house. She lights cigarettes on the front porch. She kicks the trash can when it gets empty. She sings songs to herself out of key.

"I always liked this song," she says at one point, but I can't hear the music, or the words, only the bass hum of the Alexa from the adjacent room.

A couple of hours pass and nothing on the TV does anything for me, and then the doorbell rings, maybe ten p.m., and I'm terrified as I walk to the door that it's Chase's dad finally here, but when I answer it's just Chase himself. The bandages are off his face and the swelling is still pretty bad but it all seems to have gone down a little bit.

"Sorry. Dad's tracking the GPS on my phone."

Inside, we both sit on the couch and watch TV. It gets later. At some point says that he's not sure what he wants, or that even if what he wanted once is going to be what he wants forever, and he looks at me and asks if I feel the same way and I say that I do. We both get hungry and so I pop some frozen burritos into the microwave and snag a few beers from the cooler and offer him one.

"Nah," he says. He pulls out a water bottle. "Gotta stay hydrated." I put his beer away and I crack open mine. I drink alone and we watch a movie about a giant squid taking down a cruise liner. He reaches his hand over to mine.

"I don't know," I say. "Maybe it was just one time, Chase. Just one time."

"Maybe it was. Maybe it wasn't. It feels different though. Don't you feel it?"

"I don't think I do."

"I feel it. I think. I don't know."

"Come on stop," I said quietly.

"It's true."

"Stop." I'm more emphatic.

"This scares the shit out of me, Dec. I'm trying to be honest with you."

"And I'm trying to be honest with you. I don't know what I want. I don't know."

He pulls away.

"Fine."

"Why are you here anyway? You've got a house to yourself."

He eyes me, confused.

"I came here for you. Cause I know you're lonely. That's why."

"I'll ask for help if I need it. I don't have a sign on my back. Jesus Christ."

"I'm trying to be your friend."

I shake my head. "Everybody wants to be my friend now. Everybody wants to make themselves feel better by asking me if I'm okay, if I'm hanging in there. I'm not okay. I'm not hanging in there. I'm tired of it. I'm so fucking tired of it. We're just young, Chase. We're young and we're stupid."

"Not that stupid," he says.

The TV rolls on. We don't speak. He shuffles a few times on the couch, breathes loudly. He leaves without a word. I pull out my phone ready to text Lizzy but when I open the phone the Mason account has answered.

I'm still here

"I'm still here," I say quietly.

The Liberators get their hands on something the size of a baseball and the story goes that some guy walks up from the subway line with a bomb strapped to his chest, shouting about the end, and before enough people figure out what's going on, even before some of them realize that it's not a joke, he presses a button and detonates and it's not huge but it's enough, maybe ten to fifteen people—mostly people who worked in the City from Jersey but also mothers and daughters and children and babies and the news runs stories over and over again with burnt blood on pavement and shots of debris and gray dust and the sounds of police sirens and screams.

"This is only the beginning," a voice mutters into the television screen. They whisper something about suitcase nukes, bombs homegrown in basements, and they say that by summer's end there will be a great cleaning and that "an end" is coming and even after I turn the television off and leave the room the voice still echoes inside of my head.

ⲀⲀ

We're at the rehearsal space in Asbury, lit joints and working through a couple of sub-par originals: "Cigarette Burns" and "Space Cadet" are just absolute drags. Mason even said they were when he was alive—said he scribbled those out as his first songs and he wasn't even sure why we were still playing them. We drag through the bland A/E/D progression (they're both practically the same song except "Cadet" has a capo on three). By the end Jake and I are both pissed off and so we just stop playing, end the jam with an overly loud smack of the snare and a clanging A chord.

Outside, Chase texts me and I don't answer and I'm not sure why. Outside it's quieter and the sun is hot and all of us spend a few minutes on our phones watching the videos of the bomb and the body parts and the tapes.

"Fucking wild," Jake says.

"Yeah," I answer.

"When's the next gig?" Slim asks, unbothered.

"Thursday," I answer, putting my phone in my pocket.

"Heard there might be some eyes in the crowd," Jake says.

"What do you mean?" I ask.

"Yeah," Slim says, suddenly awake. "What do you mean?"

"The band we're opening for—Ghosted—they got a record coming out in a couple of weeks. Anyway, the label is apparently hunting for new acts. They think the Ghosted LP is gonna blow up, and they want to snag up anybody who sounds even remotely similar."

"Where'd you hear that?" I ask.

"Manager at the Pony. He called me to confirm the slot. Dropped that info into the convo too."

A beat. Jake puts both his hands on his thighs and stands up.

"Let's run Mason's song again," he says, already heading back inside. A hot breeze moves in off the ocean, blowing through his hair as he shuts the door behind him.

Inside we run through the song. Slim drags. We run through it again and he drags again.

"How many times are you gonna pull us down?" Jake spits at Slim.

"I don't know, it's just fucking with me," he says. "The rhythm's so fucking simple I just don't know what to do—like I don't want to do too much it'll drown out those guitar lines. It's just too simple. You know?"

Jake takes a drag from a cigarette, a sip from the Solo cup of Svedka and tonic. "I don't know what that fucking means. Who the fuck would understand that? Who the fuck would know what that means?"

I look away. Outside the sound of thunder rumbling.

"Fine," Jake says. "Speed it up then. Descendents-style. Maybe that'll help you out."

He counts it off 1-2-3-4, maybe 160 BPM. It doesn't work and I knew it wouldn't. Slim drags. I slow it back down to the original tempo on the next take. He drags. Jake is furious.

"Jesus Christ Slim."

We play it again and again and again. Slim gives up probably on the fifth or sixth run-through—just slops his way through it while Jake and I carry him.

"Why are you so obsessed with this one?" Slim asks.

Outside Jake and I are standing on the edge of the boardwalk eyeing the storm. Dry lightning cuts through gray clouds. Dull tumbling inside of the sky.

"Let's do it," I say.

"Do what."

"Let's give it a shot. Let's play it at the show. We have to try."

Jake shakes his head. "I'm sure there's plenty of legit songs out there that never quite get their teeth into people."

"I need something. Let's take this song to the fucking stratosphere. If there's going to be some guy there, let's blow the fucking doors off."

"I don't know," he says. "I'm hesitant now. I just don't know. What if we fuck it up? Maybe it's better if we keep it to ourselves. Hold onto it. Until we know it's good. Maybe it's fine if nobody else hears it."

"I think we should try," I say.

"Do you want to come over later?" Jake asks abruptly. "Get fucked up maybe."

"What do you mean? Like me?"

"I don't know. Feels weird. Mase used to be in my house, or I used to be at your house, as much as we were at home. Feels like I should be watching out for you."

He hands me a cigarette. "I'm seeing this girl," I say.

"Who?"

"This girl Lizzy. She was at our show before."

"What's she like?" he asks. "Is she cool?"

"Yeah," I say, swallowing hard. "I think."

A beat. Jake watches the storm over the horizon. I watch the wind move over his face and I can see something like sadness, remembrance, whatever, moving through his eyes.

"Capo on 2. C to Gsus to Am to F for the verses. F to C to Gsus for choruses. No bridge—just an easy pentatonic solo. Mason knew it when he wrote it, man. He knew it was good. That's it—that's the whole song. Mason usually wrote these wild syncopated, big-dick-energy riffs most of the time, but this song is just the prettiest thing, no 7/8 shifts, no paradiddles or arpeggio accents—just slow burn beauty."

"Yeah," I say. "It was cool."

"The day he died he asked me to go surfing. That morning. I did. Out on the ocean, he asks me if I ever feel like there's something hanging over me, like a weight? Ten thousand pounds heavy, that's what he said. Asks me this as a gray storm cloud comes rolling in above and the rest of the beach clears out and it's just both of us sitting in some easy one- to two-foot lull, not talking, just being with each other, and then he leaves early and he texts later asking if I'm around. I don't answer for whatever reason. I don't—I don't even know why. The phone rang and I just saw the number and I didn't pick it up. I didn't pick it up."

A beat.

"Let's go back inside," I say, pointing to the gray over the ocean. "Storm's almost here."

Lizzy meets me on the beach. She brings a bottle of dark rum and a couple of Solo cups and a pack of Virginia Slims and a pocket JRL jukebox and she puts on The Replacements on the Sirius app and lights one of the cigarettes and passes it to me. We pass the dart back and forth and she lights another one and we pass it back and forth and it rains for a little and we sit there with the water splashing on our faces and then the rain stops. The sand now brown and wet and the sounds are distant car horns and the crash of the saltwater and the sound of laughter and whispered voices from the teenagers fumbling underneath the boardwalk. In the moonlight she looks crystalline like she was made inside of a dream but in the dark I can see the lines, contours on her face, the glisten of sadness in her eyes.

"You like it?" she says, pointing to the rum.

"My brother used to mix this with Dr. Pepper. Said it was healthy."

"Used to?"

"Before he died."

"When?"

"A couple of days ago."

"Jesus Christ. I'm sorry."

"Mason Ellis."

"What happened?"

A beat.

"You hear about that boy on the bridge?"

"Yeah," she says.

"That was him."

She takes a drag. "I'm sorry."

"It's alright, I guess."

"You can never really know somebody, right?"

"I guess."

"I wish you could," she says, more softly. She passes me the cigarette, now a stub. She pours more of the rum into the cup and sips it warm and passes it to me and I sip it warm too. She says that she wishes she had some ice and that it burns but she always thought there was something romantic about sitting on the beach drinking warm booze with a boy you'd just met or a boy you'd fallen in love with.

"You fall in love a lot?" I ask.

"Love? Ha. Hardly."

"Not your first boy you've taken underneath the boardwalk?"

She grins in the dark.

"Not the first or the last," she says. "I don't want to give you a bad impression."

"What do you mean?"

"I don't want to lead you on."

"You won't lead me on."

She laughs.

"That's what they all say. Then they melt like chocolate."

"I'll try not to," I say.

"It's the summer. That's what flings are for," she says.

"Maybe," I say, my eyes somewhere else.

"You alright?"

"It's been a weird few weeks."

"With your brother."

"With a lot of things."

"Weird with me?"

"No. I like you."

"I like you too."

She coughs out some of the rum.

"You know most dudes are trying to claw their way inside of my pants before we even get to a kiss."

"I never did that I guess," I say, a quick laugh.

"I like the company regardless."

A beat.

"You didn't know?" I ask.

"Know what?"

"That I was that kid's brother. The dead kid."

She shakes her head. "Didn't have a clue."

"I thought everybody knew."

"Not me," she says, her eyes moving toward the water.

"You're not from around here, are you?"

"We move around a lot. Dad's had a lot of different jobs. All over the place. Not sure what he does," she says. "Not sure I want to know."

"How long have you been here?"

"A few months."

"How long are you going to be here?" I ask.

"Does it matter? I'm here now."

"Yeah but . . ."

"I told you—no mush. You're inside of a moment. Stay there," she says, leaning in for a kiss.

We're on the beach for an hour maybe. We talk and drink and pass more cigarettes between us and she says that good things are in the world if you look for them but I don't know if I believe that. When we leave we sit in the car outside her house and she asks me if I want to kiss again and I do, and so we kiss. She says after that I'm good at it and she tastes like cigarettes and sugar and molasses and booze and she says that I'm soft and gentle and she wants to kiss me again and so we do and then she takes off her shirt and I take off mine and we are on the beach together under the boardwalk like the other teenagers. She pulls away after a point and puts her shirt back on and runs her hands along my chest and then she starts to leave.

I'm in the car and I'm kissing her on the mouth outside her driveway and I'm on her block watching her walk into her house. I watch a man open the door and I catch a glimpse of a head with no hair on it and he shuts the door hurriedly and she walks in more hurriedly, and then there is nothing.

Ж

At home Mom is on the couch in the living room, two empty wine bottles next to her, watching the television set, images of fire and flame and burnt skin, rivulets of orange and red and fire and crackling and screams, another recap of the subway bombing. No new leads, no new purpose: just the name—The Liberators.

I take a seat next to her and point to the bottles.

"Any left?" I ask.

"Cool it, Serpico."

"Just looking out for you that's all," I say.

"You don't need to worry."

"So is there any left?"

"In the world? Yes. Plenty. In this bottle? I don't know. Debatable."

"I meant for me," I say.

She slides her empty glass my way and I sit down and pour a handful of splashes into the wide-stemmed glass. Mom and I stare at the TV set again—uploaded pictures of what look like metal tubes, three of them, jutting out of a brown leather bag. The newscaster returns to the set and talks about a picture online, uploaded to a new account, the promise of an end. Words like *nuclear, homegrown, rising tide.* The chyron runs: *THE LIBERATORS.*

"Is it real?" I say, pointing to the tubes on the TV set.

"Hard to tell these days."

"Who are these people?"

"I don't know."

MORE TO COME

AMERICAN VIOLENCE

She mutes the TV set.

6.

Sunday is a recovery—it even says so in the Final Surge app—and I can hardly believe the terminology—maybe Taylor's getting soft. Chase texts me the moment he starts his long run and says Carter sent him a Snapchat with a hash pipe and a *"fuck Taylor"* caption. I don't answer.

Mom sits at the island drinking orange juice and coffee and holding her forehead. I point to the shoes on her feet.

"They came?"

"They came Declan," she says softly. "I'm too banged up to go out."

"Running can help."

"Maybe."

"Go for a run. It'll make one of us."

"For now."

"Just go real slow, Ma. As slow as you need to."

"Sometimes I just . . ." she starts, but then she trails off. "I don't know."

She puts her hand on my head, rubs my hair. She leans in and rests her cheek on my forehead. She fumbles inside of her shorts for a second, pulls out a cigarette, stares at it and shakes her head before lighting it. And then she heads upstairs slowly.

After a coffee I sit down at my laptop.

Leaning into the Dark

I have a vision of the story, everything except the ending—the story of Mason's life, beginning to end, unfiltered and uncensored. But the ending is . . . I don't know. The ending, like any good movie I've ever seen, like that final shot of an empty Haddonfield and the sound of Michael Myers breathing—the ending is what hammers the whole thing home, that's where the whole weight of the story comes crashing down and everything that the story can be or will be or should've been comes down to those fucking moments: what was it all about? The end . . . that's the key. Once I have that, I have everything.

But Mason's end was a nightmare.

Outside his room, I stop and look at the wood and the frame and the doorknob. It takes a moment. I'm not even sure what's been holding me back.

I limp into my brother's room. Inside the walls I imagine memories of years and decades of the people who've come before: not just my brother but the people who owned the house prior, the hands that built it, the trees that yielded the wood.

My phone buzzes with a notification, a tag in an Instagram post. Jake, facing the camera, guitar in hand.

"This is called 'Song for the Dead.'"

I remember it in its infancy, the chords bouncing off the room next to me, simple chords with a simple melody, how badly I want, once more, to run into Mason's room, throw the door open and tell him to keep the fucking volume down.

Jake plays the whole thing beautifully. The lyrics less gibberish now. Jake's lyrics now. Jake's song. Not Mason's.

"This is a song for my friend, Mason. I miss you."

I read the first of the gushing comments as they come swarming in about the beauty of the song and what a magical tribute it is and I throw the phone into the bed, stare at the 15,000 words of bullshit I've scribbled down in his memory. I catch myself crying as I watch Jake's video again. My phone dings, a text from Jake: *let's take this song to space.*

Mason points to the sky and says imagine what it would be like to fly, to drift into forever, to have nothing but light and stars and dark around you.

But then the phone dings in my pocket again: a comment on the photo I put up a few days ago, a picture of me and my brother by a lifeguard stand, the stand on Sixteenth where he taught me how to surf. The comment is from Mom, whose Instagram account I almost forgot existed. She hasn't done a thing on it since he passed. The comment is simple.

You two were my everything.

For a moment I just sit on the edge of that bed and wait for that sadness to visit again, but it doesn't. I imagine it will come again and in fact, I know it will—it always does, but for now, it's dormant, lying somewhere else. The comment comes in again, an edit:

You two <u>are</u> my everything.

I watch her walk out the front door, shoes on. She moves slowly to the edge of the driveway and stands by the mailbox for a second. She pulls one of her legs up into a stretch awkwardly and then fumbles it back to the ground. Then she starts to run. The first step is like a bomb and she goes out too hard. She moves down the block, up and down too much, limping here and there, looking broken and wounded. She's moving, one foot in front of the other.

I read the comment again.

You two are my everything.

So I grab a black garbage bag from the upstairs closet and start to clean everything up again.

Part II

7.

August first.

The storms keep coming, rolling in from the west and over the ocean—rain and thunder and lightning, rolling through the sky like sprawling hands, the air hot and wet and reeking of acid wash and cigarettes and splashes of rainbows on resin wood and the smell of saltwater taffy and bacon grease and skunked marijuana and the sound of children playing in an outdoor pool in a summer storm, and I'm on the boardwalk sitting in the rain waiting for something to happen. I find myself outside every time it rains—sitting in the cascade of water, my brain melting into somewhere else.

The rain is light and pit-pattering softly and I pull out my phone and scroll through all the Twitter stories—an abortion clinic blown to pieces in Nevada, Bill Hader going skydiving, a boy named Albert starting an anti-bullying campaign.

I sit on the boardwalk in the rain and wait for somebody to come by, and I'm stoned on a package of melted Delta 8s that I found in my glove compartment. I stare out at the water in the middle of the storm and wait for something to happen but it doesn't. I watch a runner move by splashing water in his wake. I take my shirt off and sit there in board shorts in the rain and the rain doesn't stop. Sounds move like snakeskin and the color of water comes in undulations and waves.

In the car later, Chase opens the door, an hour past, sits in the passenger seat. I'm soaked, rain pouring off the bangs in front of my eyes. He watches me as I look out the window.

"You alright?"

"Fine," I say.

"Sorry I'm late."

"An hour late."

"Parents don't let me out really since they found us. Had to wait for them to go out."

"Where are they off to? The local Klan meeting?"

"We're going away for a while. Down South. The house in Tampa. Dad says it's better there."

"Why there?"

"He says it's safer."

"The Liberators," I say.

"I don't even know what to think."

"I don't either."

A beat.

"We're leaving tomorrow, Dec."

"Okay."

"You want to go out tonight? Get stoned?"

"Not really."

"Why not?"

"I don't know."

"What else are you doing?"

"I don't know."

"I don't know when we're coming back, Dec."

"Yeah."

"Before the school . . . before a while I guess."

"You'll be back."

"You want to go out though? Let's get drunk. We don't . . . let's get drunk somewhere out. Let's go to the arcade and get drunk."

"I don't want to go to the arcade and get drunk."

"Why not?"

"I just don't."

"Sorry."

"You don't have to be sorry about anything," I say.

"Yeah but . . . "

"It's fine."

"Alright."

"Yeah."

"I'm gonna go."

I turn and face him.

"Yeah," I say. "Okay."

"Maybe we'll be back soon."

"Yeah maybe."

"Dec . . . "

"Yeah."

"Never mind."

"Okay."

Then he leaves. I watch him vanish into the rain. The rain gets louder, louder, until it's falling in sheets on the car. I can't see him as he vanishes into the blue. I can't even see the ocean anymore.

At home, I'm on the couch with the TV on mute and staring at the phone in my hand, the last text I sent the Mason account.

I'm thinking about you right now

The dot-dot-dot lights up. Vanishes. Lights up again and vanishes. Nothing comes back.

✗

I'm drinking from the Poland Springs bottle I filled with rum at home and I don't even really bother to hide it and I get pretty drunk. The rain keeps coming outside and it feels like maybe it will never stop. Mom must start to smell it on my breath after we order in Chinese food and sit at the countertop and eat. She pulls the bottle out of my hand, sniffs the contents, and takes a sip.

"Gross," she says, handing me the bottle back.

Outside the rain turns to thunder and lightning, concussive rumbles in the distance.

"I saw the song that Jake put up," she says.

"Yeah?"

"That was Mason's right?" she asks.

"Yeah."

"Did you and Jake—"

"Yeah we talked about it."

"Okay," she says quietly. "A lot of views."

"A hundred K, I think."

"Some local buzz. *The Asbury Park Press* called."

"They did?"

"To ask about him."

I shake my head.

"We didn't know what to do with it. I didn't think he was gonna . . . just record it. It was a song for the band."

"Seems like his song now."

"No," I say. "It's still ours. It's still ours and Mason's."

"Okay," she says.

She moves her eyes to the urn above the fireplace.

"Nobody's called yet," she says, after a moment.

I don't answer.

"About Mason. About finding his body."

Background noise of the television: a convenience store blown to smithereens in one of the Carolinas. One of the toothy-grinned newsplastics uses the words "American violence" over and over again and at some point runs it as a chyron: "American Violence." *American Violence.* The phrase sticks. They play some of the videotapes The Liberators have been dispersing online: images of fire and rain and hail and violence, a flag fluttering in the wind. The news stations call the voice narrating each of these videos The Queen, an appropriate title for the crackly, near-royal intonations that proclaim each threat.

WE ARE ALREADY HERE

I listen to her voice coming through static visuals, purring intonations and promises of a new world order. She says that something much worse is coming. She says that the world is nearing its breaking point and they will be the ones to shepherd us into Judgment Day. "*Change is coming*," she hisses. "*Devastating change*." I listen to her and the sound of the cicadas outside.

Devastating change.

8.

We're supposed to be on at about 5:30 p.m. At home, before I leave, I run through "Song for the Dead" over and over, sipping from a frozen bottle of Cuervo, hitting the snare too hard and slamming the bass drum with too much ferocity and leaving subtlety somewhere else. At this point I've shed the boot—the pain is still there, loud and clear, but I don't care anymore. It'll heal or it won't, who gives a shit.

In Asbury, security outside is meaner and more aggressive and the pat downs are harsher but they don't care about the booze and the weed and the pills people drag in—more on the lookout for knives and ARs and bombs and whatnot.

Jake passes a joint backstage and I chase down the smoke with a couple sips of the Cuervo and Jake gestures for me to pass it to him and I do.

"Hundred thousand views dude," I say.

"Yeah," he says. "Crazy right?"

"I didn't know you were gonna record it like that," I say.

"I just wanted to get it out there in some capacity. Before it vanished."

"Let's keep it our song man. Alright?"

"Alright."

"I'm serious," I say, sharper than I wanted.

"Yeah," he says after waiting, taking a last hit. "Of course." His eyes lock on me.

He leaves. I sit and finish the tequila. The show starts.

On stage, Slim drags through "Cinnamon Girl" and he fucks up some of the other originals we have and then when I get to "I Wanna Be Sedated" he manages to make that sound somewhat respectable. I see the sound tech giving the *get off the fucking stage* hand signal and Jake ignores it, takes a drink, and calls for "Song for the Dead." He slams the C.

"'Song for the Dead.' Slow and sad," he shouts.

Before anybody can protest, he walks up to the mic. I count it off. The song starts with the guitar part this time.

It moves through the sad and the slow and Jake fills in more lyrics but this time they seem set in stone, like the ones on the video, and I'm too drunk to know what he's really saying, but I know it hurts, and Jake's voice cracks here and there and at some point I notice that the crowd is starting to get kind of quiet, the kind of quiet somebody gets when they're watching something happening and it *feels* like something is happening. I hit the snare hard as I can, keep the bass drum skittering beneath it, and ride the hi-hat quiet. The crack of the snare drum skittles through the air beneath the flange, wet sound of the guitar. I don't know—as he's singing, even for three minutes, for the first time since Mason's been dead, he feels even, for a second, alive in the words and the chords and the way the sound bounces off the ocean in the distance.

The crowd erupts afterwards—the way a crowd isn't supposed to erupt for a song they've never heard before, let alone for some jerkoff opening slot at some jerkoff venue.

I imagine Mason standing in the crowd watching, dead now—his eyes gray, his skin sloughing off, his body bloated and decaying.

The Ghost.

At the bar with Jake the bartender tries to push us away but Jake hands the guy something in the palm of his hand and then we both have Svedka and tonics in front of us and Jake passes me mine and cheers and we both take a sip. This dude dressed all in black, flickers of gray hair slicked back in that kind of Brylcreem look, comes up and introduces himself.

"Victor."

I reach out to shake his hand. He ignores it.

"You guys sound pretty good," he says, eyes on Jake.

"Yeah, thanks," Jake says.

"This your band? Where's the other guy?"

"Who the fuck are you exactly?" I ask.

He chuckles, points to the name on the card he hands me. *Victor Price.* "You ever heard of me?"

"No."

"Those originals in the middle of the set?" he asks Jake.

"Yeah."

"They weren't good."

"Thanks," Jake says.

"What was that song at the end?"

"That was ours."

"My brother's," I say.

"You write it?" he says, eyes still to Jake.

Mason explaining why the G sus was the best chord before the Am.

"Why does it matter?" Jake asks.

"Did you write it?"

"No. My friend did. Somebody else in the band. My friend's dead."

"What's your name kid?" Price asks, still on Jake.

"Jake."

"Who's this?" he points to me.

"Declan."

"And the dead kid?"

"His name was Mason."

"And he wrote that? The dead kid?"

"Yeah."

"Damn good."

"Yeah."

"A better story is how you wrote that song for your dead friend, in tribute to him, you know, his memory and all that. Now that's a story. That's a story that maybe fuels a hit. And hits these days, especially in middling soft dick alt-rock, hits are few and far between. And now, with all the world going to hell in a handbasket . . . you might have a little window. Song for the Dead. Nice title. Fortunate timing."

"Fortunate?" I spit.

"Let's try this again," Price says, eyes still on Jake. "Did you write that song?"

A beat.

"Yeah sure," Jake says. "I wrote it."

I pull back.

"That's better," he says.

He fingers the toothpick in his mouth, then leans in.

"Ditch the bass player. Kid's an amateur. Then give me a call."

He vanishes into the fray. I pull on Jake's shoulder.

"What was that man?"

"Do you want the song in the world or not? I heard there were gonna be eyes here and now there are eyes."

"Mason's song, man. Our song."

Jake shakes his head. He takes a breath, looks like he's composing himself. "He's dead and gone. In a minute, an hour, next week . . . he'll vanish. They'll have some tribute for him at Mass in September. They'll say a prayer. Maybe Mrs. Smith will make us write an essay on him. They'll talk about him at graduation. And then it'll just be that. He'll just be something we think about every couple of months, every couple of years, and then never again. He'll die and he'll just get absorbed into all the other sad fucking deaths in the history of all sad fucking things."

Jake finishes his drink.

"This is him forever," he says. "And it probably won't work Declan. It won't work. But this is how we keep him alive. Isn't that what we want? Him? Forever?"

He leaves me there, alone. I wander out into the crowd, blend into the scene. I close my eyes and picture myself inside of a balloon, floating into the sky.

Ж

That night I Uber to the bridge where Mason died. I have the guy just drop me there on the side and I get out and the guy gives me a strange look and asks me if I'm okay and I say that I am and then he leaves. I light a joint and stand by the wilted roses and the ribbon and the name tag and the picture of Mason. I stand there on the edge and peer over into the black beneath and the blue run of the Manasquan River and I try to imagine myself falling and what it must have felt like near the end, the hesitation and the fear and maybe even the bliss and then the fuel for all my insomnia in the past few weeks: the body tumbling downward to the saltwater washing itself over with those first waves of guilt and doubt and begging that it wouldn't hurt and hoping he could survive and feeling the speed increase and knowing just how many bones would splinter upon impact and how they'd have to plaster your face back together and how you were so smashed up and broken that Mom wouldn't let me see you and how one night we got stoned on edibles and went down to Bradley Beach, played mini golf. Mason won, sunk a hole in one on the twelfth hole, with the windmill and koi pond.

"Motherfucker! Sometimes I even impress myself."

Later, on the beach, he passes me a beer he snuck from the garage.

"It's gross," I say, taking the first sip.

"It's an IPA."

"Bleh."

Then we smoke another blunt and he says that the moon is freaking him out and he wants to go for a walk and so we walk toward 71, inland and south, and some of the time walking we don't talk and some of the time walking he just hums a song but I don't sing along cause I don't know the words.

"Check it out," he says, pointing to this derelict house sandwiched on the western side of Sylvania Ave, barely into Neptune township, five or so minutes from the water, right where the WASP-y part of the Shore ends and the harder part begins. He'd told me he wanted to show me something.

"Used to be an orphanage," he says, pointing to the sign: Seashore Family House.

Mase says that the owners died a few months back, that they were old people and that they used to house kids in here, and that you can tell by the flowers on the walls of some rooms and the football helmets on the walls of other rooms.

"Do you think this was a good place?" he asks.

"What do you mean?"

"Do you think this was a place where they helped kids?"

I don't have an answer. He keeps speaking.

"Maybe it was. I hope it was. I hope it was where like boys and girls woke up every morning and felt something . . . felt like they were loved. Felt like they could go out into the world and make magic. Do you think that was this place? Or was it something else? Like a bad dream. Do you ever think about that?"

"Think about what?"

"How just in the world . . . right now, outside your window, maybe a hundred feet from where you're sitting, there's somebody living in the worst kind of pain, the worst kind of misery, somebody who doesn't know what they did to deserve it but wakes up every morning feeling like the entire weight of the world is breaking them to pieces. I think like that a lot. I don't know where it comes from. I just can't shake it some days and this place reminds me of that."

"You told me once after Dad died. You said you just felt things then. The world. All of it. The good and the bad."

"Like you're plugged into the wall and there's just too much heat and electricity and it blows the whole circuit. That's how I feel sometimes, Declan."

"You alright dude?"

He smiles. "Always."

We walk around the empty hallways for a while and Mase takes pulls from the handle of Banker's and I keep wishing I had water for both of us instead. He runs his fingers along the wall. In one room there's a broken jack-in-the-box. He pulls it open and the toy keyboard makes a few half-hearted, off-key bleeps before dying out completely.

There's a sledgehammer in the living room, the dusted imprint of a couch and chairs where lived lives used to be. Mase halfheartedly takes the sledgehammer in his hand, brings it down gently through the floor. The wood cracks and splinters easily and then he seems to regret it. He passes me the thing and I hit a few floorboards. Mase attacks a wall with some fury. Floral patterns explode into sawdust and drywall. He keeps at it for a while but then just stops and he says it seems stupid, and then he asks me if he thinks people live forever, even after they die.

"I don't know, Mase. I hope so."

"They chased me out of religion class once. I told them that eternity sounded like torture. Like the idea of something going on forever without an end—bonkers. Completely fucking bonkers. Now I'm not so sure."

"Well," I say. "I mean, the odds are stacked against us right? Somebody will be alone someday. Even if just for a little. That's just . . . I don't know."

"That's how good stories go though, Dec. The odds have to be against them, right?"

"Yeah I guess."

"Well, I hope we don't separate for too long. Maybe we will. But I hope not."

"And just think man . . . if we do, we'll have spent years together. Years. We'll be part of each other's memories forever. So even if we're apart, we're together."

"That sounds good," he says. "I like that. Even if we're apart, we're together. Forever."

On the bridge I send off more texts to the account. It doesn't even matter what I say. I write and write and I wait for the reply, the reverb and the slapback and the echo, and none of it comes, and the account is silent and dead like Mason. I think about tossing my phone into the water. I don't. I stare out from the bridge at the water in the east and imagine the sun rising and rising and getting hotter and hotter and burning away all the things inside of the day and inside of the night and all the space between blood and water.

9.

Lizzy comes over later that night. Before she gets there, I watch from the backyard, Mom inside of the house opening the fridge, shutting the fridge, wandering around the house. I watch her as she searches the house for something, anything, nothing.

Lizzy and I sit by the pool in the backyard and listen to the sound of the crickets and she passes me warm Corona and a couple of Marlboros and she puts on Bon Iver and we pass the cigarette back and forth and we drink beer and she asks me questions, pulling peels from an orange. The night is warm and humid and damp and everything sits heavy on the night.

What do you want from your life?

What do you want to see?

Where do you want to go?

What do you want to learn?

She asks questions and I give clipped answers and try to feel some kind of honesty, but she persists, asks gently and asks more gently the next time. Sometimes we kiss and she tastes like nicotine and sweat and tongue. I scroll through my phone and one time she asks me what I'm looking at and snatches the phone from me. She points to the Twitter headline about a new strain of Ebola spreading in South America, whether it's a natural mutation or a bioweapon. She turns the phone off and then she kisses me again and we kiss for a while. She asks me if I'm okay and I say that I am and then she keeps kissing me. I can hear the sound of thunder in the distance and everything turns to gray and noise, my stomach rumbling as she fumbles with my belt buckle and then there's a voice like "hey" cutting through the air and when I look up there's Chase, standing in the backyard too, hands in his pockets, head down.

"Who's this?" Lizzy asks softly, pulling away.

"Hey," I say, buttoning up.

"Never mind," he says, hands still in his pockets, vanishing back into the dark of the front.

"Wait," I say, standing up. Lizzy reaches for me but I'm up and moving and she says something to me as I follow Chase into the front yard.

In the front of the house, I watch Chase sprinting down the street, hailing the Uber he just called. I chase after him and call his name and he turns and slows down and then we're on the street.

"Hey," I say.

"It's fine. Don't worry about it," he says.

"Dude wait. Please wait."

"I'm fine," he says again. He checks his phone, taps his foot nervously. Dry lightning across the night sky.

"Chase. . . ."

"Whatever man," he says. "Like you said—just one time." I want to speak, to say something, but I don't. He shakes his head, walks further down the street. I don't follow him. I watch a car come to a stop next to him and I watch him tap on the glass and then I watch him get inside and as he drives away, another streak of dry lightning across the night sky. I stare at the car as it vanishes into the dark and into the black and the lightning cuts through the dark in the sky.

In the backyard, Lizzy is behind me, hand on my shoulder. She kisses me on the ear.

"Who was that?"

"I don't know. Just my friend."

"Your friend?"

"He didn't know about us. He's just been tight with me forever. Gets flustered."

"Seemed perturbed."

"You could say that."

I shake her off when she tries again.

"I'm tired," I say.

"Let's go inside. I can stay. I'll stay."

"I said I'm tired."

"Okay," she says, standing up.

"Sorry. I'm just tired. I promise."

Ten minutes later I'm inside of the house, sitting in my bed, staring at the ceiling in the dark, a half-empty bottle of Cuervo that I've brought up from the liquor cabinet next to me. I take a pull and stare up at the ceiling. I'm out of drugs now. I stare at the ceiling and wait for the shadows. I rap on the walls above my bed waiting for a ghost. I rap on the walls. Nothing comes.

I walk downstairs and wander the house. Everything is clamped and quartered and tight.

Outside the house I stare at the streetlights and wait for a shadow to move underneath them, to catch a glimpse of a face moving through the night. It doesn't come.

A text message splits through the fog what feels like minutes later, maybe hours. My screen lights up. The same account from before: *@mase_314*

Do you want to know why I died?

ꭗ

The next morning at breakfast I don't tell Mom about the message or Chase or Lizzy or any of it and I watch her pour a glass of orange juice and another and figure her head hurts as much as mine. She sits at the marble countertop and stares at the glass in front of her and when I figure she's not going to make anything for herself I get up and go to the fridge and grab some bacon and some eggs and some wheat bread and some Kraft cheese and fry up the bacon, fry the eggs in the grease, fry the bread in the pan and make her a sandwich. I cut it in half and pass her the plate and she grabs half and passes me the plate back, gesturing for me to eat. I pour her a coffee and pour myself one and sit down next to her.

"You drink too much?" I ask, sliding the cup in front of her.

She nods, takes a sip. "Becoming a habit."

"Me too."

"Want to do something today?" she asks.

"Like what?"

"I don't know. Anything. A lot of time without a gig," she says.

We sit there for a moment and don't speak and she takes another bite of her sandwich and I take another bite of mine. She stops like she's thinking about something and then leaves me in the kitchen alone by myself. The sun pours in from outside and the heat strews off the hardwood floors. My head hurts.

She comes back in the room with a little pink bag in her hand that she tosses my way. I read the label—açai-flavored. I look up at her.

"Come on Dec. Let's do something fun."

"You want me to get stoned with my mom."

"Yeah," she says, a smile.

"I mean. . . ."

"Don't be a scrub. You want to get high and go to the beach with your mom or what?"

ꭗ

She brings some of the boogie boards from the garage when we walk to the beach and we both strap some beach chairs to our backs, and she puts some water in the mini-cooler packs on the back of each chair. We walk slowly and she asks me, in a kind of panic, whether she's going to freak out and I ask her if she's ever done drugs before and she gives me a look and a harrumph and keeps walking and I say that if she just focuses on bright things and sunlight and the smell of hot dogs and doesn't get scared she'll be okay.

On the beach we sit close to the water and she reclines back and the sun is hot and for a while we just float away and then she asks me if I want to go in the water.

She splashes around on the board pretty good and catches a couple of waves and one wave knocks her off the board pretty bad and she laughs for the first time since Mason as she's getting tumbled in the sea. She gets confident and attacks another wave and this time she doesn't even make it past the crest and gets absolutely flattened before she can dive underneath it. We sit on the sand after and she doesn't speak for a while but the smile stays on her face for a while before it leaves. When it leaves, the same expression from the days and weeks before settles in and we're quiet on the sand watching the water splash up on the shore.

We walk across the street and eat some pizza and she says she's ready to go home and so we go home and in the house she pours herself a seltzer and asks if I want one and I say no. She finishes it pretty quickly and says that she'll order some food soon, just needs to sit down, and then she goes to the fridge and pours herself another seltzer and leaves some room at the top and then she pours the Svedka on top and grasps the glass with both hands as she takes a swallow and she closes her eyes and takes another sip and then I watch her walk outside by the pool and sit and for a moment I just watch her sitting there finishing her drink and wonder what she's thinking. She comes back inside and makes another one and she finishes half of it before she goes back outside again and then I don't have to wonder anymore what she's thinking.

I sit on the couch and look at the messages I haven't answered from Chase and Lizzy, the chyrons, the pictures from earlier in the summer. The day moves by.

A Corona goes empty and then another and then another and I swim in the pool water for a while, float on one of those inflatable recliners, spit chlorine water up in the air, watch the sun start a slow descent and keep getting drunker. The phone buzzes on the table. I don't answer it. I catch some caterpillars migrating across the concrete and I flick them into the pool, feel bad, scoop them out, put on *OK Computer,* and stare at airplanes in the night floating way off in the distance and imagine them all crashing into open fields. I dive in the water to cool off the booze.

When Mase used to play beer pong he'd usually win by dropping his cock on the table and fucking up whoever's shot. When I open my eyes under water he's flashing me, a few weeks ago at Brandon McIntyre's party, one of the ones Mase and Jake had actually invited me to.

"Fuck you dude. Put that fucking thing away," I say, rubbing my eyes and spitting out the water. When I open my eyes he's gone.

I spend the night getting as obliterated as I possibly can, sitting in the basement and staring at the mauve walls and watching horror movies on TV. Mom comes downstairs and asks if I'm hungry and I say that I'm not and she looks at me flatly before leaving. I finish the pack of Coronas and make my way to some more Cuervo and I don't even bother mixing it with anything but ice chips and I'm on the couch, watching a movie about some family that gets stranded in the mountains and eat each other alive and I eat a bunch of pretzels and pour another tequila and stare at myself in the mirror, tan skin and abs and stubble, my ankle still swollen. I pull out my phone as everything starts to get hazy and text back the *@mase_314* account.

tell me what you know

When my head starts to hurt I lie down on the couch downstairs and try to close my eyes. The room spins. I get up and move to the bathroom and throw up and then I'm on the tile floor with the lights on and when I realize I'm not going to puke again I turn the lights off and I sit in the dark of the basement bathroom listening to the air moving through the house. I squint my eyes into the dark and try to imagine a ghost standing there, a body—what it would be like to be Mason peering in from the other side and watching me. I imagine his eyes locked on me and a rush of cold moves through my blood underneath my skin and I stare out into the dark waiting for something. Maybe I can call it something—the feeling that I'm not alone, the messages from beyond, the *tick-tack-tick* of the rattling air conditioner that seems to score the eeriness inside of that basement.

The Ghost.

That's what I can call it—The Ghost.

My eyes adjust to the dark and I can make out shadows and shapes and the outline of the couch in the basement and the foosball table wedged into one of the corners, a layout of Yankee Stadium posted up on one of the mauve walls that now look like walls of dark.

Go into my room

Look under the floorboards

See what you find

The next morning, I wake up to the messages I've missed overnight. I walk upstairs into the kitchen and pour an orange juice and chug it and walk upstairs to the shower. I jerk off and hop in the shower and stand under the steam for a while and when I'm razzled enough I walk out into the bedroom and change and stand outside my brother's room listening through the door, listening for what I'm not sure but just the sound of the air passing through and hearing the emptiness in the spaces where there was once fullness.

I head inside the room and look around at the tomb and walk on the hardwood floors and listen to the sound of the creaking and the way the wood moves underneath my feet. On the air, the same musk of nicotine and sunlight and sweat from life and the soft smell of mothballs and dust and stillness that came when he died. I walk over each floorboard slowly and when I get to one it bends underneath my foot, like it's about to crack. I pull up the floorboard and siphon through the bag of dead weed and a lighter and a scribbled set of song lyrics and a couple of warm cans of Coors that Mason had wedged underneath. I rifle through the song lyrics looking for something, anything, and I'm about to stop when I come on a page that doesn't look like the others—not the scribbled ramblings, zigzagging lines of before or the musical annotations or the chord progressions or all of the other splintered thoughts. Just what looks like a note, written to somebody, written in the form of a letter, only a few lines.

> *When I die, I want to become immortal. I want to live forever inside of dying. I want to be everywhere and nowhere at once. I want to be in the dirt and the sea and the air and I want to exist inside of everyone's dreams at the same time, and when one person is thinking of me, everybody is thinking of me. I will be gone, but not gone, not dead, but alive, somewhere inside something else forever, inside of some other form of existence.*

I sit down on the edge of the bed and read the letter again. What he could've meant, when he wrote it, whether he knew what he was planning on doing when he wrote it, questions now. I text the number back.

Who is this? For real?

It's me. Mason.

It's not you. You died.

Then where's my body?

Floating somewhere in the Atlantic.
Food for the crabs.

That current from the river pulls right into the ocean, right by the coast. I would've washed up weeks ago.

It's not you.

I want to believe more than anything that I am lying. I want to know that he's somewhere, anywhere, even if he never sees me again. I want to know he's breathing, eating food, staring at the summer air, drinking a warm beer, listening to the Stone Roses and flicking embers in the air. I want to know he exists in some space somewhere.

I didn't die Declan. I didn't jump off that bridge. You know it and I know it. I'm still here. That's what that note meant. I am not gone.

I am not gone.

Fuck you. This is bullshit. Prove it to me. Tell me
something only Mason would know. Anything.

Come on motherfucker, tell me something.

You there?

Mason?

10.

Jake asks me to come over, says that we have something to talk about, and so I get showered up and make my way out the front door. I ride my bike to his house—down Ocean Avenue through the heat of the summer and past the pizza joints and the ice cream shops and the Dunkin' Donuts and some of the bennies from Staten Island cavorting on the side of the street and pointing towards the parking spots they've illegally hijacked. Jake lives on the other side of Belmar closer to Spring Lake and it only takes me a handful of minutes to get there and then I'm on North Boulevard, looking out at the lake, knocking on his front door. He lives in a small house that sits on the corner of the ocean and the water. His money came from his dad too—another Wall Street boy who came and went—and his mom was one of the kinds that found herself into recreational Valium and fortune telling and fates and all of that. Mason used to say that she'd have the tarot cards spread out on the table every night at dinner and offer up some prescription for what doom lay around the corner and how Jake would just tune all of it out and how Jake's brother Elijah would just tune all of it in.

Jake opens the door, tank top and board shorts and cigarette.

"Come in dude. You won't believe it."

Inside he walks me through the hallway into the kitchen. His mother is at the countertop with a glass of orange juice in front of her, hair frazzled, skin so tan it looks like leather. She nods to me and I walk past without a word and we go downstairs into his basement. I'd only ever really been over when we'd had practice or when Mason had me pick him up when he was too drunk, and I have stayed away from Jake's mother for as long as Mason has told me story after story about Jake's mother.

In the basement he passes me a cup of coffee and lights a cigarette and pulls the Takamine sitting on the wall and starts strumming through chords again.

"That Price dude wants us to bag Slim."

"What do you mean?"

"He called again. Said we *have* to bag him. Said he'll find a bass player when we need it."

"I mean Slim's been with the band for a while."

"Yeah, but he sucks."

"But he's still been with us awhile."

Jake shakes his head.

"I don't know. Seems like a door is opening and we want to walk through it."

"Maybe."

"He wants more of you on the track too," Jake says after a beat.

"What do you mean?"

"He just thinks it's like a singer/songwriter-type song and he thinks if you're going to be in the band you should contribute more a little bit. You hold back until the second chorus and even then it's just mostly accents. He thinks maybe you should come in on the second verse. A more steady beat."

"A more steady beat."

"Yeah."

"Okay."

"He got us a slot at his studio. Thursday morning. He wants to give the song some proper treatment."

"It just seems like it's moving really fast."

"It is. Maybe that's how it goes."

"Yeah."

"Can I ask you something?" I say.

"What's that?"

"Before he died . . . did Mason ever mention anything? About dying? About . . . running away maybe?"

"Running away?"

"Yeah."

"No. I mean Mason couldn't hold any thought down for real long. You know that. He bounced around a lot. Why do you ask?"

"I found something. A letter he wrote. To himself I think. Maybe to me. I don't know."

"What did it say?"

"I don't know. It doesn't make sense."

"You sure?" he asks.

"It's just he's dead. I know he's dead. But there was no body. They never found him. And . . . I just need to see him. I need to see the body."

"Yeah I get that."

"Do you still talk to him?" I blurt out.

"To Mason?"

"Yeah like . . . in your dreams. Or messages for him on Instagram. Stuff like that."

"Yeah," he says. "I have this . . . I mean, I don't know. I hear him every time I play this song. And I have this—I talk to him sometimes."

"Where?"

"Like I just imagine myself talking to him. I sit there and I have these dialogues in my head with him. Sometimes I even say the words out loud. I respond like him. I don't know. It's stupid."

Jake looks down at the guitar.

"Yeah," I say.

"You know I know I'm being kind of belligerent about this song," he says.

"A little."

"I just . . . like, he showed me this thing. He showed you it. It must've meant a lot to him. It must have meant enough that he wanted us to have it before he died. Some form of it."

"I guess."

"So I'm just trying to honor that I guess."

"I think it was all bullshit," I whisper.

"What do you mean?"

"His whole schtick. It was all an act. The freethinking independent rock-and-roll dude. The contrarian. Just an act. Couldn't hold down a thought and couldn't hold down an opinion because he didn't even know what any of the big ideas behind his opinions actually were. Empty words. Just emptiness. That was Mason. Emptiness."

Jake strums lightly on the guitar, blinks.

"That's a little harsh," he says.

"Yeah, well, he died. That's harsher."

Jake doesn't answer and I wonder if he thinks he shouldn't. Instead he works his way through the chords again, hums along to the melody.

"When we come in on Thursday—maybe have something mapped out for that verse and chorus. Something a little stronger. Price thinks this song has enough as it is with the guitar and the vocals. So you want to make sure you're making your case."

"Making my case?"

"Yeah, man. I want you on this journey, right? For your brother."

"Jake."

"Yeah."

"Are we sure about this? Laying this song down. I know you're fired up about it. I guess I am. It just doesn't feel right. It doesn't even make sense. Sniped out of a crowd by some A+R exec?"

"It's what Mason would've wanted."

"It what's ***you*** want too . . . ," I whisper.

"Isn't it a dream? Isn't it a way to give your brother's story some air?"

"I don't want his story to have any more air. I want it to go away. I want it all to go away."

"What else are we supposed to do?" Jake says, leaning forward. "Seriously man. What else did he leave us with?" Jake shakes his head. Since I've known him, he's been quiet and calm and stoic, an antidote to everything helter-skelter that defined Mason. But in his eyes . . . now there's something that looks familiar: that abscess that Mason left us, that schism.

"Okay, Jake," I say. "Okay."

We work through the song a couple of times and I just play the beat on my knees. Jake nods along when I come in on the second verse but focuses on the chords and vocals. We work through it again and again and again. Jake's nods progress into smiles and by the end he looks at me with something like pride. The song sounds good, I'll give him that. Beyond that, I don't know.

"It's good," Jake says when we're done. He comes over and ruffles his hand in my hair.

"Yeah," I say, pulling away.

Upstairs I pass through the main hallway lit only by the morning sun and try to sneak my way out of the house, but on my way there's a shadow coming out from the kitchen. I follow the shadow for a reason that I can't quite explain and I see his mother has a set of cards laid out in front of her on the kitchen table—tarot cards, all arranged in some kind of a hexagon. She moves and sorts them around in various slots and I stop for a second in the hallway watching her move these back and forth with passion and energy and then she catches me staring at her. I cannot remember her clean in any sense of the word, ever.

"I didn't see you there," she says, eyes back on the cards. Her skin is taut and tight and pulled back like she's made of leather, like you could unzip her straight down the seams. She has a blue and white chiffon on, and she waves the baggy arms around like she's casting some kind of spell.

"Sorry."

"It's nothing to be sorry about. Come here," she says, quiet and breathy.

I walk over to her, and she gestures to come closer, and I do and then she points to my hands. I lay them in front of her and she takes them in her hand and turns the palms up to face her. She threads her fingers along the lines in my palms and she traces the ridges and the valleys and the cracks and she breathes very softly as she's doing it and moves slowly along the pathways. She bends my fingers back slowly, each one individually, checking for something whose measure I'm uncertain of. She brings her fingers to a stop at the center of my palms and looks me in the eyes.

"What do you see?" I ask.

"What do you want me to see?"

"I don't know."

"Sure you do."

A laugh.

"I don't really believe in this stuff," I say.

"Everybody believes in something," she says.

"Fortunes and fates," I continue.

"Then why are you still here, with your hands in mine?"

She smiles, runs her fingers along the pathways again.

"You can leave if you want. You can leave anytime," she says.

A beat.

"Tell me what you see," I say, more softly.

"If I tell you there's a snake waiting in the grass outside that's ready to strike, ready to hurt you, even kill you, that your hands tell me that there's that snake in that grass just outside that front door—you'll walk out that door anyway. You'll go looking for that snake. We all want to interrupt fate. We all touch the hot stove. Because if you don't find it, then I'm a fraud and a fake. You'll go home and you'll tell everyone you know about the crazy lady just down the street. But if you walk outside and the snake's there—you'll believe in the unbelievable forever. You'll believe in all the things we cannot see or quantify or make sense of. You'll believe the world doesn't make sense. Those lines on your hand are just another way of sorting it all out, all that swirling chaos."

I shake my head. "Magic isn't real," I say.

"Your brother believed."

"You didn't know my brother."

"He believed. Living and dying. Life after death."

"You only know so much," I say.

"People who do that to themselves . . . it's not just about them. It's about what they leave behind. It's about the knowledge of how much they're going to torture the people they leave behind. How much suffering they're going to cause simply by being absent, and by raising questions—could I have done something differently? That's magic. That's life after death. That's eternal legacy—even if it's a torturous one. You don't think he knew that at the end? You don't think he knew what he was leaving you with forever? That sweet torture."

"Fuck you."

"I don't mean anything by it," she says. "I'm just reading the signs. It's all bullshit, right?"

A beat.

"It's just lines on a hand," I say. "And you're just a lady in a kitchen."

She actually smiles.

She goes on. "I remember you as a boy. Chasing around your brother. Running after him like a child chasing a truck. I remember wondering what you were running toward.

What is it like now? Where, or who, are you running to now? Or are you still—chasing a ghost now?"

I shake my head.

"I remember you at the kitchen table at breakfast. Half asleep before noon. Passed out by lunch," I say.

Jake steps up from the basement stairs, suddenly visible.

"Everything okay?" he asks.

A beat.

"Fine," I say. "Everything's fine."

Jake stares at both of us. I turn to leave. His mom speaks softly as I turn toward the door. She catches my wrist with her hand.

"I'm sorry things turned out this way. I really am. And I am sorry for what is coming."

I turn to face Jake, but he's already gone back down the stairs. We are alone.

She turns back to the cards on the kitchen table and begins shuffling them again. I stay next to her for a beat and leave without a word when it's clear enough she isn't turning to speak again. Outside I sit in my car and drive to the boardwalk and watch the wind move across the water and the ripples forming in the blue. I watch a gust blow the first of the leaves off one of the trees adjacent to the shore and I watch some of the leaves, burnt and brown, drifting over the path and skating over the water, the first infinitesimally small hint of fall and decay and death and the end of the summer on the back side of the vinyl.

XX

I'm home and the storm clouds roll in again and I'm staring at the television smoking a joint. The woman on the TV set talks about The Liberators and a camp they found in the middle of New Mexico and a website with strange messages and riddles in it and something about a countdown embedded into the website's code and how the countdown stopped at midnight on Labor Day.

"What is the clock counting down toward? What is coming? This and more later . . ."

I'm stoned so I walk outside and sit by the pool and listen to the buzz of the pool filters. I stare up at the sky and imagine a flash of white light and surging heat and a curtain being drawn. I try to hear anything above the sounds of the night and the hum of the filter, but it all sounds alien and tight and vacuum-sealed. I scroll through the phone—a financial crisis on the horizon in the winter, a tsunami, fentanyl in hand-rolled cigarettes.

Tell me about that message.

Tell me what you meant.

I wait for the answer. No dot-dot-dot. No promise of anything. I run my hands through my hair, tap my foot on the ground, wait for something. Nothing.

Tell me why you died.

Where did you go?

Where are you now?

He is six years old stretching his arms out toward the sea. He is ten years old, pointing to a baseball gliding over the left field wall. He is seventeen years old, a guitar in his hand, a cigarette in his mouth, green inside of his eyes. You are each of these moments, both alive and dead forever, inside of me.

The boy is maybe ten years old, standing in front of me, shaggy black hair. Next to him is another boy, blond and clean cut. They both have that kind of handsomeness that only a natural shithead can muster. This is my memory of a day, just one day, perched inside, a record on loop. He flicks a quarter with his middle finger and his thumb at the boy with the blond hair. The boy with the blond hair becomes the boy with the guitar in his hand playing the music of a ghost. The boy with the black hair becomes the ghost.

"You want to play some music?" the black-haired boy asks. "I'm Mason. Who are you?"

"I'm Jake."

I am the boy in front of them both on some summer morning. Was I there the moment they met? Did I write this memory in my head? Did I design the story so the puzzle pieces fit or did the puzzle pieces fit in a way that fit the story?

He flashes in and out of focus like a frame vanishing from a film and soon he will be gone forever and the movie will run on loop without him inside of it and the journey will run in circles without a main character, without a protagonist, running in circles with the hero lost forever.

11.

I TEXT LIZZY AND TELL HER TO MEET ME somewhere and I hop on my bike and cut to the intersection at Ocean Avenue and turn right and head toward Spring Lake. I stay on the sidewalk and pass the drunks and some of the vagrants. I'm too stoned and all of the sound cuts in and out like knives and each word or phrase or conversation sticks like putty and I hope that Lizzy brings some booze to calm me down. I scan through some of the Snap stories, a couple of the runners at Carter's house and some girl in Point Pleasant who's having a Robots and Sluts mixer and Chase . . . Chase just with a photo of the Atlantic Ocean from Islamorada. The ocean in his shot—black and white—soft waves crashing on the beach that shimmer like monochrome glass. I reply to the story with a thumbs up and I wait for an answer but it doesn't come.

Lizzy and I find each other on the pavilion. The moon is out and a breeze cuts in from the ocean and I'm on one of the benches facing the ocean, my hair whipping behind me. She pulls up on a beach cruiser and parks it on one of the rails and makes her way to the seat on the bench and wordlessly passes me a Poland Springs bottle with dark liquid in it. I take a sip and take another big sip and the whiskey is almost half gone before either of us says a word.

"You alright?" she asks.

"Maybe."

"You don't seem alright."

"Just jittery that's all."

"Anything you want to talk about?"

"No not really."

She palms the bottle and takes a sip.

"I snuck it from my dad's liquor cabinet," she says.

"You know, I hadn't even heard your name before. I grew up around here. I knew everybody around here. I didn't know you."

Her eyebrows squint.

"I told you. We move around. I come and go places. It's nothing serious."

"I just hadn't heard of you."

"You don't know everybody around here. You don't know everything. We just met, my dude."

"Did you know him?"

"Who?"

"My brother."

"No."

"Are you sure?"

"Yes I'm sure."

"Not at all?"

"Declan what are you talking about?"

I shake my head. "I don't know. I've been talking to him—"

"What?"

"My brother. I've been talking to my brother. Not really him. Just somebody online."

"What are you talking about?"

"There's an account. It's been sending me messages. It says it's him. And I've been talking to him."

"You've been talking to your dead brother."

"Yes. Well no. It's not him. I know it's not him. Lizzy I know it's not him. I just . . . It feels good to talk to . . . some version of him, some approximation of him. Cause it's his voice, well not his voice, but it's . . . in my head I can *hear* his voice . . . and it . . . when I say it to myself or when I hear it in my head it's his voice. You know? It's his voice."

"It makes sense."

"People say that. They say 'it makes sense' or 'I understand' but they don't. It's just window dressing. Nobody understands. Nobody knows what it's like to have somebody do what he did. To leave that hole. Those questions. Like a grenade. Nobody knows."

"You're right," she says. "I don't know. I know what I found though when I met you."

"Some fucked up narcissist," I say.

"Fucked up yeah," she says.

"Self-absorbed prick."

"A boy who just lost his brother."

I shake my head.

"This was supposed to be a good summer," I say. "Before senior year they say that's when high school really starts. The parties pick up. People can drive. But now there's just me. And Mason."

"Have you said goodbye yet?" she asks.

"At the funeral I think I said goodbye."

"Yeah but like *really* said goodbye?"

"No. Because I'm still talking to him. On my phone. Every day."

"Then I think you need to delete your phone. Or throw it into the river."

"I just need things to get better. And it feels like everything is getting worse. Like imploding. Like the world absorbed all of Mason's life and is breathing it in like poison."

"Maybe your worldview has just been corrupted."

"No shit," I say. "You found me at that show."

"I found you at the show because I took a couple of edibles and biked down to the Pony to see who was playing. I don't know anybody around here Declan. I'm a transplant. My nights . . . I'm home. With my parents. My dad mostly. And when he's not too sick I'm out at the shows or I'm on the beach or I'm hooking up with you."

"And then there's this feeling . . ." I say.

"What feeling?"

"Like I'm being watched. Like there's something near me. Somebody. Maybe it's the text messages. Like a ghost."

"A ghost."

"Yeah."

"You're just worked up. You're hurting, Declan."

"Yeah, but I'm not losing my mind. I can just feel it—like he's still here. Still inside the house. Still inside the walls. Still watching me. Watching all of us. You know like when a lightbulb bursts . . . that flash of light and how it gets caught in your eyes for a second. Stays inside of your eyes even in the dark. An echo. That's Mason now. An echo. Somewhere. A ghost."

"Declan . . ."

A beat.

"I don't know what's happening. I don't know why he died. I don't know what the fuck is going on with my band. I don't know anything."

"Declan."

"I just . . ."

The words fall away. I stare at the water and everything goes blurry.

"Declan . . ."

The tears come warm and quick. I cry into her shoulder, and she pulls me close.

"You're okay," she says. "You're okay."

I wipe my eyes, pull back.

"Nothing's okay. Fuck."

She kisses me on the forehead. She holds the kiss and pulls back. I can smell the perfume on her neck, vanilla conditioner in her hair. When the tears stop, I lean into her neck. I lean hard into her neck and then I'm kissing up to her cheek and her mouth. She pulls back hesitantly but then pushes in and we kiss more and then she's asking me for the car keys.

We're in my bed later, my eyes on the ceiling. She runs her hand on my chest.

"Did your mom hear?"

"I don't think so."

"Was it your first?"

"Maybe."

"Come on. Tell me."

"Yeah."

"Ah look at that. Another one taken."

"How was I?"

She shrugs.

"I've had better."

"Fuck you."

She laughs, kicks my feet under the covers.

"Shh . . ." she says, her pointer finger over her lips.

"She's asleep. She'll stay asleep. You can sneak out the window in the morning. There's a . . . rhododendron. Something like that. Right beneath."

"I'll boogie when you pass out."

"I don't sleep much anymore."

"Yeah," she says.

"So how many before me?"

"Two? Three?"

"Bullshit."

"What do you mean bullshit?"

"Bullshit," I say, smiling.

"Not in the least. Three, I think. Yeah. Three."

"You seem . . . more relaxed than that."

"You've just got a dumb view on women. It's actually possible to not exist in binary forms. You don't have to just be a whore or a Puritan."

"Fair enough."

"Who was the first?" I ask.

"Boyfriend a year ago."

"Where was the old place?"

"South Jersey. Near Absecon."

"Atlantic City."

"It's where my dad grew up. This is my second stint in Jersey."

"What was the boyfriend's name?"

"Jack."

"How long?"

"Like two minutes on average, four on a good day," she says.

"No like—fuck you. How long?"

"We dated for a year."

"Why'd you stop?"

"I moved."

"Why'd you move?"

"Dad got sick."

"Sorry."

"Yeah, so am I."

"How sick?"

"Cancer sick. Stage four. Words like sarcoma."

"He's dying?"

"Not dead yet."

"And you and Jack."

"Dead."

"Harsh."

"I cut it off. Not a long-distance girl. Love comes and goes."

"You didn't even try?" I ask.

"I'm from everywhere. I've lived . . . Virginia, North Carolina, California, Oregon, now Jersey again. Everything comes and goes. And I don't like breaking hearts. It's all too messy."

"Nobody does."

"Some of it's avoidable. Some of it's just living. This is the avoidable heartbreak."

"Is that me too?"

"Nah. No heartbreak."

"Really?"

"It's not that serious," she says, smiling. "We'll be toast by the end of the summer. Two weeks max."

"Maybe I don't want to be toast."

"But we will. I'll make sure of it. This is a summer fling. This is something out of a movie. And the movie will end."

I put my head on her chest.

"Maybe I don't like that answer," I say.

"Well, be that as it may, it's still the answer."

"Had a lot of leaving this summer," I say.

"I'm not leaving this mortal plane. I'm just going to stop sending you nudes."

"You haven't sent me any nudes."

"Yet."

"Tough to stop sending them if you haven't started."

"Maybe tomorrow."

"Yeah?"

"Yeah."

"After breakfast. After a big breakfast. Before I even can take a shit."

"Fuck off."

A beat.

"You know . . . it's only been like five weeks. Everything's just tossed upside down," I say.

"Since he died."

"Yeah."

"How'd you find out?"

"He talked to me before he left. He said . . . just said he was going out. I found a note on his pillow. I brought it to Mom. She called the police."

"Sorry."

"If he died, I'm not even sure the fall did it. The water broke his ribs maybe. Broke some bones in his face. Broke his shoulder. Maybe drowned. Maybe he was unconscious. But yeah . . . he drowned. Dying alone. Choking to death. Without me. Without Mom. Did he think about me, you think? Mom? What was his last thought? Did he regret it? All for nothing. All for bullshit."

I pause.

"Or he's still out there . . . texting me from the grave. No more Mason. No more Dad."

"What happened to your dad?"

"Vanished. I was three or four. Just up and left. Died a few years ago. Somewhere in Los Angeles, with a whole new family. Left us a pot of cash though. Kind of a parting gift."

"You've had a fucked life," she says.

"Yeah."

"I'm sorry."

"I don't need pity."

"It's just sad."

"Who gives a shit?"

"Nobody should have to go through that."

"I don't want to talk about it anymore."

"Okay. What do you want to talk about?"

"I don't want to do much talking."

"So what do you want to do?"

I reach under the covers and put my hand on her stomach. She laughs, wraps her legs around me, and climbs on top of me. She leans in and kisses me again. I pull her closer. She whispers something under her breath and reaches under the covers and everything starts again. She moves more slowly this time and so do I and seconds become minutes and minutes feel like hours and warmth becomes heat and breath turns ragged.

Before it ends a knock on the door and then the door is open. Mom stands in the frame of the doorway. She eyes both of us, our sheets now pulled over our bodies save our necks and heads, pauses a moment.

"Out of my house," she says softly, then shuts the door.

Lizzy leaves out the window in the next five. I hear the crunch of the rhododendron. I wait for Mom to come back and talk but she doesn't. I wander into the hallway looking for her and when she sees me moving towards her room she stops for a moment and shuts the door softly.

ᚷ

I wake up naked at six in the morning, the sheets off. I watch the orange cut in through the window blinds and the way that some of the streaks of light cut through the dust in the air floating like plankton. The morning comes slow. I open the window and catch the heat of the breeze as it cuts through the air.

In the shower I clean off last night and wash out the salt from my hair.

I'm in Mason's bedroom again. I'm in his drawers rummaging through old empty dime bags and a couple of broken cigarettes inside the desk. I scan through pages of song lyrics, mostly scribble, mostly unrelated jabber and chord progressions and a couple of doodles on the side of headless people and bulging eyes and scatterbrained color schemes. His cellphone sits on the desk and when I try to turn it on nothing happens, so I plug it into the charger that's still wedged into a ball by the checkered pattern of his bed. I stare at the battery icon on the screen and wait for the familiar white of the Apple logo and then Mom is standing in the doorway, looming in front of the morning sun behind her.

"Who was that last night? The girl you brought home."

A beat.

"Listen, we don't have to stand on ceremony."

"Just some girl."

"Quite a pivot from last week."

"Yeah, well it's been quite a month, hasn't it?"

She shakes her head.

"Were you smart?"

"I'm always smart."

"You know what I mean."

"Yeah, I was smart."

"Please not in my house again."

"Okay."

"I'm asking nicely."

"And I'm answering nicely."

A beat.

"You're being an asshole, Dec."

"I'm coping."

"You're being an asshole."

"Well you're being a drunk."

"You wore a condom?"

I point to one of the drawers on Mason's desk.

"I used some of his. There's still some left."

"Hell of a legacy," she says.

I shake my head. "Well what are we supposed to do with them? Donate them to Goodwill?"

"What's her name?"

"Lizzy."

"Nice girl?"

"Sure."

She looks around the room.

"I don't like you being in here."

"Why?"

"Because I don't. It's his room. And I don't want you in here."

"Mom, it's not haunted."

"The whole house is haunted Declan."

"Oh Christ Mom."

"On that note . . ." she mutters.

"On that note what?"

She half-smiles.

"I'm putting the house up."

"What?"

"Yeah. We're selling this house."

"What the fuck? When?"

"ASAP. I've got the money. I'm . . . I have no desire to clean this place. Been through enough. But there are people who can. You remember Elise from church?"

"We don't go to church."

"Well . . . when we did. You remember her. Elise. She used to bake the oatmeal chocolate chip cookies—bring them in for the bake sales and whatnot. Anyway. It's what she does. She stages houses. And so, she's coming here. Full cleaning crew. I told her I'd pay her whatever."

"Wait—you're serious?"

"Yeah, I'm serious. Up on September first."

"Two weeks."

"Two weeks. And this place will fly off the shelves."

"Mom what the fuck."

"Come on. It's just a house. No I mean . . . I understand but . . . Declan this is hard for me to explain. I can't stay here. I don't know. The way things are. I just can't stay here, I don't think. I don't know."

"It's the house I grew up in."

"It's also the house where your dad up and left. It's the house where I raised you two alone. It's the house where your brother died. That's this house."

A beat.

"And we're leaving in a few days."

"What?"

"You and me. We're going away for a while. I told Elise she can stage the house while we're away."

"Where are we going?"

"LBI."

"For what?"

"To get away."

"You got a place?"

"Yeah. Found one on AirBnB."

"Where?"

"LBI."

"No shit. Where?"

"Beach Haven."

"How many arms and legs did that cost?"

"Several."

"What if I don't want to go?"

"I don't give a shit. You're coming with me. I'm not . . . you're coming with me. I'm not leaving you here alone."

"We're heading into the city soon. To record that song."

"Be that as it may . . . you're coming with me. You and I are going away for a couple of days."

"When are we leaving?"

"Friday morning. I've got it for the weekend."

"Maybe I'll come."

"Maybe?"

"Maybe."

"No maybe. Who the hell do you think you are?"

"I don't want to go."

"And I said I don't give a shit. Now get out of this room. Get out."

She walks in and makes a shuffling motion and pushes me off the bed. I head out into the hallway and she shuts the door behind her.

"Put some clothes on," she says.

Downstairs later she is on the couch with her eyes on the television, sounds of violence. She sits there idle and I stare at her somewhere in between heartbroken and furious and lost in the moment between now and before and today and yesterday and memory and reality and Mason is a boy now, staring at the kitten that's been run over outside of our house, its body limp and its fur splashed with red curled up on the side of the road, on the edge of the sidewalk, as if it had crawled there to die alone and—

"What if I died?" Mason asks Mom, in that moment.

"Then I'd find a way to be with you."

"Be with me where?" he asks.

"Wherever you were, I'd find you. I'd find you."

On the beach later, I smoke a joint and stare at the waves crashing onto the edge of the shoreline. Jake texts me and tells me that we're headed into the city tomorrow and that he can drive me and that Price says we should come ready to be there the entire day.

You sure about this? I text Jake.

Yeah.

Think of how great it's going to be. For Mason.

I sit on one of the benches on the boardwalk and watch the families tumbling by and I'm higher than I wanted to be so I walk down to the Playa Bowls on Ninth and sit inside the faux tropical, bohemian café and eat granola and açai out of a plastic bowl. I roll another joint in the bathroom and smoke it on the corner by Fletcher Lake and walk up to the bench again. I watch the sun on the water and the light reflecting off the green-blue of the waves and the heat rising in shimmering rivulets from hot sand and the way the air smelled like a memory and the breeze felt like the sound of sepia tones. Motorcycles and Camaros and old Chevrolets roll by with the windows down and the sound of jangly guitars shining out from rolled-down car windows and the smell of rubber burning on hot asphalt buried inside of summer songs.

I'll pick you up at 7. We can drive.

I stare at the message from Jake and punch a thumbs up emoji back.

At home, I open the laptop and stare at the words in front of me: *Leaning into the Dark.*

On the morning that you die, you wake in the bed that you've slept in since you were a kid. You stay in bed as long as you can—every step today is a march closer to the end. You think about the choices . . .

I highlight the whole thing and hit Delete.

"Fuck."

I text the handle again.

Are you up?

I wait for a bit and the dot-dot-dot lights up for a second, vanishes. Lights up again and vanishes.

Yeah.

What are you doing?

Just hanging out. I need breakfast.

Where are you?

I can tell you that later. Not yet.

Frustrated, I shake my head.

Are you safe?

Yeah man. Totally safe.

How can I believe you?

You'll just have to try.

While I'm texting I'm staring at the document where his story is supposed to be. Ten K words roughly—just scribblings. I'm talking to him on the phone, some imitation of him.

Tell me something I don't know.
Tell me a secret about Mason.
Something only he knew.

The dot-dot-dot lights up, vanishes.

I didn't want to die.

Sure you did.

Everybody makes mistakes.

Then what was it like

Dark. Loud. It hurt.

You drowned. In the river.
Did you feel yourself drowning?

I didn't drown. I didn't die.
It's just what you want to hear.

I don't believe you.

I was out. Knocked out from the fall.
Broke my bones into pieces.

I still don't believe you.

You don't believe anything I say.

Why should I?

Do you believe you're talking to your brother?

Most days no. Some days.

What about today?

No. Today I think it's bullshit.

Then who am I?

Some fucking hacker.
Some cocksucker halfway
across the world in bumblefuck.

And you're still talking to me.

Prove me otherwise.
Prove it's you. Prove I'm talking to a ghost.

What do you want to know?

Something only Mason knew.

A beat. Another beat. The dot-dot-dot lights up and vanishes. Stays quiet.

You and I fought on the night I died. We fought. More than a normal brother fight. Something uglier. We said ugly things to each other. I left the house angry at you. That was the note we ended on: anger. Ugly anger.

Mason left the house and left a note and then he killed himself. I tell myself that the conversation we had on the night he died was the same kind of conversation we always had, the same ribbing back and forth that sits between brothers and how it wasn't anything out of the ordinary.

But it floods in anyway: the image of my brother standing at the edge of the doorway, his face contorting into a scream and his finger pointed at me and the spit that spat from his mouth when he pointed his finger at me and in my memory the words stay on silent and I can just see his face and imagine my own spitting back at him.

Fuck you.

You wanted a secret.
You got a secret.

How did you know?
How do you know?

Because it's me, dude. It's Mason.
How many times do I have to prove it to you?

I send this denial back into the chat but I already know the lie. Inside of a memory I stand up and take the biggest step I can with my left side and chuck a glass of water into the wall across the room. I watch splinters of glass jettison from the side and hear the sound of the shards hitting the floor. Mason stands in the doorway screaming and I stand across from him and I watch myself like it's a movie screaming back at him and I imagine the sound from downstairs, how the bass echoes of our battle would reverberate off the walls. We'd fought a thousand times before and we would've fought a thousand more times but now we're stuck eternally in the absent resolution we didn't give each other.

I'm out by the pool with a warm glass of whiskey in my hand and I'm staring at the whiskey and trying not to drink it. It is hotter than it has been the last few days. There is no wind on the air. You can hear the buzz of the emptiness on the air.

Mason crashes into the water—

I finish the drink and have another. It can't be much past noon. I have another and another. In the shallow end of the pool, I watch the caterpillars scurrying across hot concrete and falling into the water and they struggle and float and twist on the surface, rippling timidly beneath their fluttering, and then they sink under the water to die. I watch them struggle. They claw their way to the side of the pool begging for a rescue. I don't offer one. The struggle wears off and they drift slowly beneath the surface, carried away by the current of the filter, and then it's the night and I am watching Mom as she shuffles around the house trying to find minor things to do, bills to pay or dishes to clean or doors sitting ajar that need to be shut.

I am in bed staring at the ceiling and watching moonlight cascade off the top of the ceiling, mauve and gray and shaded by night. I listen to the sound of the air conditioner turning off and on, eyes on the shadows above me.

And what was it like when you died? I imagine her asking this question to the dark at night. How does she answer? Can she answer? Is it even something anyone can conceive of? A child is born and a child grows into a boy and then the boy is gone. The boy is the child inside her heart and in her mind. Is this all she has now to visit? Memories and gravestones and dead fireplaces inside of cold winter.

I am a boy sitting inside of a memory and I think maybe I will be stuck inside of the memory forever.

12.

In the car on the way to the city, not even six hours later. My head is pounding, my eyes bloody, my skin flushed, muscles dull and aching. At six in the morning the alarm had gone off and I'd hit it asleep before I'd even known what the sound was and then it was seven o'clock and the sound of the heavy pounding on the front door, Mom at the edge of my doorway telling me to get up and then I was downstairs with a cup of coffee in my hand and Jake telling me we had to leave five minutes ago.

In the car he doesn't speak and he puts on the demo tape of Mason's song and mouths his way through the lyrics as we careen down the Turnpike. The sun splintering off the hot metal of the front hood of the car and I put the air conditioning on as high as I can and recline, open the passenger side window and ask Jake if he has a cigarette. He hands me one and then it's the wind whipping through my hair and the smell of nicotine. Streaks of white across the sky and the hot air blowing down from the north.

"You nervous?" he asks.

"I don't know," I say.

"I think it'll be cool. No matter what happens. It'll be good."

"Sure."

"You alright?"

"I'm fine."

The Ghost sends the first text somewhere around eight a.m. when we're stuck at the Holland, maybe a quarter mile out from the dull black of the tubular entrance.

Do you want to see me again?

Do you want to meet?

"Jake."

"Yeah?"

"Do you believe in ghosts?" I ask, as we pull into the tunnel.

"What do you mean?"

"Ghosts. The dead. Hauntings."

"No. Why do you ask?"

"No reason."

"Come on tell me."

"I've been getting these text messages. Say they're from Mason."

"You told anybody?"

"No reason. Think about the amount of spam calls we get in a day. All of us. Same thing."

"You think this is really Mason?'

"No," I say. "I mean they never found his body."

"Dude."

"I mean they didn't."

"I know man but—"

"No I know. I'm not stupid. I know he's dead. I just—"

"It's just some scammer. Some bullshit scammer."

"So where is he . . . if he's dead?" I ask.

"Mason."

"Yeah."

"He's gone."

"Forever?"

"The curtain draws. It goes black. There's nothing else. And better for it. Think about it. The relief."

"You really believe that?" I ask.

"As much as you can imagine."

"I don't."

"Why?"

"Ghosts, I guess."

"You're just broken up."

"I'm not."

"But you are."

"No. I'm just talking it out."

"Have you seen him since he died?" he asks.

"No."

"Then you're not losing your mind."

"I'm not."

"Okay."

A beat.

"We'll be there in half an hour or so."

"What are we doing anyway? Making some half-assed attempt to hit it big?" I say.

"It's not half-assed."

"This guy's a prick."

"All music execs are pricks."

"Yeah? You an expert?"

"I mean . . . I don't know. Right? Comes with the territory."

"He seemed like a giant prick."

"We don't have to do this," Jake says.

"It's a little late now, don't you think?"

"You sure?"

"Couldn't be more sure."

"It's not even that hard of a drum part. You don't have to do anything."

"Thanks for the vote of confidence."

"It's not what I meant."

"It's fine."

"It's your brother's song dude. I want something good to come out of—"

"Nothing good comes out of it. There's no romanticizing it. There's no swelling music, no Solsbury Hill, none of it."

"Jesus Christ man I would've left you home if I knew you were going to be such a fucking downer."

"Downer. Yeah. Sorry when I woke up I didn't pop enough beta blockers."

"Jesus Christ man."

"Let's just sit here. Let's shut the fuck up, disassociate for a little bit, and sit here. We can walk into the studio and be all hunky dory but for a moment, just a moment, can everybody just shut the fuck up and let me be. That's all I want. I don't need to win the lottery. I don't need people to bring my brother back from the dead. I just need people to leave me the fuck alone. Leave me alone. Fuck off. Fuck. Jesus Christ. Fuck."

A beat.

"Okay sorry."

"Let's just shut the fuck up," I say. "Let's just shut up and drive."

So we do.

ж

Victor meets us on the corner of Bleecker and Sixth. He asks us where we parked and Jake starts talking about some parking garage around the corner and Victor just brushes him off, says we could've taken the train, says that only tourists drive.

"Follow me," he says, wiping the sweat from his brow and smearing it on the front of his shirt.

We move past the tourist bars and the CVS and the joint with the pirate ship out front and Victor waves to a couple of random people that walk by and says their names out loud like he knows them. They wave back mostly and then he asks if we're hungry and he says that he's hungry before we even answer and he pulls out a wad of cash from his pocket and walks into one of those sidebar pizza joints populated on every street corner and orders us a couple of pepperoni slices.

"You vegan or something?" he asks me when I'm just picking off the pepperoni.

"Don't like pepperoni," I say.

"Ah," he says, taking a bite. "Thought you were one of the vegan types. Gluten-free. My wife is into that. What happened to the other guy?" he says, turning to Jake.

"Let him go," Jake says. "Like you said."

"Good."

"Hey, don't you want to get to the studio?" I ask, pushing my plate aside.

"You in a rush?"

"No I mean . . . who's paying for this? Are we?"

Victor sets his eyes on me. "I'm the one paying for this. We can take our time."

"Okay."

"You can relax, you know."

"I'm fine."

"So who's the one who wrote the song?" he asks. "I can't even remember it if I'm being honest. The story or the song."

"My brother," I say.

"His brother," Jake says.

"And he's dead?"

"Yeah," I say.

"How?"

"Jumped off a bridge."

"Yeah? Jesus Christ. What a shame. Fucking shame. It's a good song?"

Jake and I lock eyes for a second.

"Yeah it's a good one," Jake says.

"Must've been for me to book you. I don't book just anybody. I'll come down the Shore here and there. My wife's dad has a house in Bayhead. Anyway. The Shore. Good music scene sometimes. Not like here. The Shore . . . mostly wannabes. Has-beens. That carnival sound thing, you know? But I'll go. Check out a show or two. Not really even chasing rock and roll so much anymore. Where'd rock and roll go? Nowhere. Just nowhere. Rap. Hip-hop. EDM. All this stuff evolved, like it or not. Where'd rock go? Nowhere. That band you loved ten years ago is hocking Van Halen covers now and playing the festival circuit or grabbing bands just like them and hopping on a booze cruise three times a year to pay the bills. Jesus Christ. Meal plans and sobriety tours and exercise regimes and all of it. What happened to rock and roll? It's like a fucking traveling band of Mormons. Fuck. But I booked you. You must have something. I don't even remember. I hope it's good. Sorry about your brother. Was he a good guy?"

"Yeah," I say.

"Fuck it. Let's get out of here. Get it over with. You guys certainly know how to make conversation. Does anybody know how to make conversation anymore?"

He walks us a little bit further down the block, always a few paces ahead, and then we're at the foot of a beat-up wooden door wedged in between a deli and another pizza joint. Victor fumbles with the keys for a little bit before finding one and almost ripping the door off its hinges as it opens. We walk up a set of musty stairs barely lit by flickering fluorescent lights hanging from above like a makeshift fish tank. At the top a single red door at the end of a narrow hallway and then he opens the door and we're inside a studio even dimmer and less bright than the hallway that preceded it, an engineer behind a soundboard and a transparent pane, a couple of lit candles and the smell of skunk weed and an array of guitars and basses and one set of drums lying around. Victor plops himself into a reclining leather chair and kicks the wheels back so he's jammed up against the wall and then folds one leg over the other and sort of just stares at us.

"Ballad, right?" he says.

"Yeah," Jake answers, head down.

"How'd you play it when I was there?"

"What do you mean?"

"The instruments. Acoustic. Electric. How'd you play it?"

Jake fumbles.

"Uhh . . . I mean, I was on guitar. When Mason was alive . . . he was lead. So it's just—I mean without Slim it's just—"

"Keep it simple."

"I had a Tele. Me and the vocals. Slim was on the bass. Declan here on the drums. Mild distortion. A little flanger. Nothing really. Some reverb maybe. I can't remember."

"Yeah," Victor says, nodding, somewhere else.

"You want us to lay it down?"

"How long was it?"

"I don't know. Three, four minutes."

"Any solos?"

"Mason used to take one. I did when you were there. Slim turned the fuzz up on the bass. Covered it a little. Sounded kind of empty though."

"It'll sound emptier on tape. And solos . . . I mean, who cares. Nobody likes solos anymore. Can you play the keys?"

"No," Jake says.

Victor looks at me.

"You?"

"No."

"Neither can I," Victor says. He turns to the engineer behind the panel in the other room, shouts.

"Rich! Keys?"

Rich, the guy, whatever, nods his head.

"Just a few notes," Victor says. "A quasi-solo. Something like a bridge. Will been good."

A few minutes pass and we sit pretty quiet while he sets up the equipment around us and decks out the room, sets up mics for the bass drum and the snare and the high hat and threads the plug from Jake's guitar into a Marshall stack in the corner. He asks Jake to play a few notes and he does and Victor just shakes his head, says the distortion's too crunchy and re-plugs into a Fender amp with some orange fuzz run through it.

"Anything else?" he asks, eyes on Jake.

"A little flanger."

"Alright."

He fiddles around with some of the pedals a bit and Jake runs through a couple of chords.

"A little delay maybe," Jake says, suddenly sheepish.

"You tell me what you want, and I'll do it."

"Yeah," Jake says. "Some delay. Cathedral reverb."

Victor nods and leaves the room for a second, comes back with another pedal and threads it through, fucks around with it for a little bit, asks Jake to hit a few notes. Jake runs through a couple of chords and the sound is good and everybody nods.

Victor turns to me and sort of sizes me up and down.

"What's the BPM?"

"I mean, I don't know."

"The tempo. What's the tempo? I don't remember."

"I don't know. Slow burn—maybe like a hundred?"

"A hundred isn't a . . . you're a drummer right? A hundred? Come on. Slow burn is like down in the seventies. You sure you're up for this?"

"Yeah. I'm up for it."

"Rich!" he says, turning around. "Click track like eighty-one. Something like that." Rich gives the thumbs up.

We're decked out in headphones and separated by a pane of glass and Rich asks if we can hear him through the phones and we both nod. He asks me to run through the toms to make sure they're good and I do.

"Alright Jake—you next," the voice comes from inside my ears.

Jake runs through a few more chords. I can't hear much.

"Hey, can you turn him up?"

"Yeah," Rich says, giving the thumbs up.

"I just want to be able to hear the song."

Victor leans into the microphone and taps it. "You don't want it too loud—the click track's what you should be focusing on. How many measures before the chorus?"

"I mean, I don't know," I say. I eye Jake through the glass. He shrugs.

"Do you guys have any set structure here?"

"I mean, no. I guess. I mean we've only played it a few times."

Victor holds his hand over the microphone and turns to Rich and starts mumbling something. I don't hear anything but the muffled sound of both their voices. Both their heads shake and Victor smiles at one point. Then he pulls his hand off the mike.

"Alright just take it from the top. Run through it once. See what you got."

There's a thumbs up and I can feel my stomach inside my throat and I'm not sure why and then Rich says that there'll be an eight count before the recording begins and then the familiar click of the metronome is in my ears. I eye Jake through the glass—who goes first? And he sort of just shrugs and his eyes are as dizzied as mine and then we're four beats away, three, two, one . . .

Jake's first strum is clumsy, gets caught along some of the strings and it just sort of scrapes in my ear and before he can even get to the G there's Rich again inside our ears.

"Relax," he says. "Just relax. It doesn't have to be perfect. We're not selling perfection."

I don't know what he means but before I can ask any questions the click starts again and then we're back. Jake hits the first C smoothly this time and then moves to the G and suddenly we're rolling. I'm in the background mostly, working the ride cymbal a little bit and keeping the tempo with the hi-hat. When the first chorus rolls around, I pick it up a little bit and when we get back to the C for the verse I come in and sit behind.

A song for the dead

A song for tomorrow

A song for forever

A song for forever

I imagine I should feel something in the moment, like some kind of pride for injecting Mason into some version of immortality, but all I feel is something like apathy and mild disgust and by the time I get to the second chorus I'm actively hating the entire process and thinking about ways in which I can fuck it up. I start pounding on the bass drum and smacking the snare and with each line of the chorus and with each breath that Jake takes I try to up the ante behind him more and more, turning what's supposed to be some sloshy, sad ballad into trashy Lars Ulrich. I keep my eyes behind the booth the entire time and I can tell Rich and Victor don't feel it and I'm waiting for them to cut the track but we just keep going and there I am, playing along to a ballad like I'm fucking Neil Peart.

The song ends and I finally turn through the glass to look at Jake who's sort of just staring at me. Victor and Rich come into the room and for a moment nobody says anything and then Victor sort of just shakes his head.

"So should we do that one again?"

Afterwards, we're down at the same pizza joint we started in, the night now, Victor sitting in front of Jake and I, this time with a lit cigarette and a joint that he's passing between all three of us. There's sweat on his brow that seems like it's been there since we entered the studio. His eyes are bloodshot and his skin is that kind of tan-dark seeping with booze.

"That was good. I don't know how it started. Wasn't expecting much. But it's good. It's really good." He points to both of us, raises the joint like he's offering a toast, and then takes a drag.

"Thanks," Jake says. "I'm just glad you took notice."

"Yeah kid, me too."

"What's next?" I ask.

"What do you mean? After this?"

"Yeah."

"You go home. I go home."

Jake leans forward.

"Do you want us to come back at any point? Like . . . I don't know how it works. Do we get to hear a rough mix at some point? Something like that?"

Victor takes a long look at both of us.

"I'm not following," he says.

"For the record," I say. "When do we get to hear it?"

"When it's a hit," he says, laughing. "If ever."

"I don't get it," Jake says. "I'm sorry if we sound ignorant. I just don't get it."

"What's there not to get? You did your part! You did a great job. I'm excited to see where it goes. There'll be a check in the mail shortly, and maybe one day down the road, there'll be a bigger check in the mail."

"What?" I say.

"I don't think you understand this arrangement," he says. "I'm sorry if I wasn't clear."

"Clear about what?" I say.

"I mean, I'll be blunt—this isn't your song anymore. This is how it works. There's a lot of artists out there, big and medium and small, searching for a hit. And maybe they could've written one ten, twenty, thirty years ago but the engines just aren't turning anymore. That's where you guys come in. I happened to be down at that bar and I heard you play and I thought maybe you had something. I do it all the time. Not just I, to be clear. The business. Listen, it's a great song. Don't get me wrong. The credit will be—well, I can't guarantee that either, sometimes they pay off pretty handsomely—listen, the song may exist in some form, someday, somewhere. It's got a chance. That's the best I can offer."

"So that song, that recording . . . none of it is for us? The band?" Jake stares at Victor like he's got two heads.

"Us? What is 'us'? What are you talking about? You guys are . . . I mean, you're nice kids, but you're nobodies. Nobody wants a nobody hit. We pay for the hits. That's what happens. No blossoming artists are crawling up the Hot 100 anymore. All of them are bought and packaged and sold like . . . like the word *organic*. Think about that word. Organic is everywhere, right? However many years ago it became a phase and then a trend and then a hot commodity and stayed in high demand. There's nothing that's actually organic. It's just packaged that way, so it sells. It's the same thing with music or art or film. There's no independent artistry, there's no rags to riches, there's none of it. There's just money. And I saw green when I saw you guys on the stage—green for me, green for Rich back upstairs, and yeah, maybe a little green for you."

"Jesus Christ," I mutter.

He passes me the joint. "Take a drag, kid."

It all feels so fucking absurd that I oblige him and take the biggest drag I can. When he reaches for the joint, I stuff it back into my mouth and take another drag. He shakes his head, chuckles.

"I'm not trying to be cruel," he says. "It sounds like a real sad story what happened to your brother. Really. And maybe if he were here, he wouldn't have sold me that song. But you guys did. All that paperwork you signed on the way out the door? What do you think that was? You read the fine print at all?"

Jake and I eye each other.

"I mean," Jake says. "No."

"No. Exactly."

A beat.

"So what now?" I say.

Victor shrugs halfheartedly.

"We bid each other adieu. You go back down the Shore. You keep playing shows, doing the circuit. Maybe you tell somebody you wrote a hit song. Maybe you get some girl to fuck you because of it. It's all hunky-dory. Only catch is . . . just can't play that song anymore. Another part of the paperwork you signed. At least until I say you can."

"Wait, what the fuck? Why not?" I say. Jake motions for me to calm down, even extends his hand over to mine and I push it away.

"Declan, that's your name, right? Irish name. Full of piss and vinegar just like any good Irishman. You're heating up a little. Listen to me. That song is good. It might even be real good. Good enough for somebody bigger than you or bigger than your friend here—Jake, right?—to take a bite. And I don't need you guys parading it around as yours."

"It is ours," I say.

"Not anymore," he says, almost mournfully.

"I didn't think . . ." Jake starts, then just trails off.

"Listen, man, I'll send over the paperwork tonight, okay? You can see what you signed. I'm not in the business of being shady. I'm an open book. I'm just letting you know that it is not in your best interest to be parading that song around, monetarily speaking. How many litigations can a bunch of frat boys get caught up in, right?"

The joint I've had in my hand starts to sputter and fade. Victor reaches across the table and takes it out of my hand, snuffs it on the countertop. He looks around the place for a while like he's searching for something.

"Listen," he says, reaching into his jeans, "here's some cash. There's a bar around the corner, Rusty Nail, that doesn't ID anybody. If they do just say you know me. Sit at the bar. Have a drink. There's an old-fashioned they make with cocoa bitters, and they use mandarin peels that they've smoked. It's really . . . it's top-notch, I'm telling you. Anyway have a drink. You touched greatness. Really. You did the thing. Most people chase it their whole lives. You guys are what? Twenty? And you did it. This is a proud day for you guys, nothing less. A proud day."

He throws a couple of hundreds on the table and stands up.

"I'm glad we ran into each other," he says. "I really am. That's a great song you guys came up with. A really great song. Proud to be a part of it."

He says the last part as he's turning away.

"We'll be in touch, I'm sure. I'll see you around."

Then he's out the door. Jake and I sit inside the joint staring at one another, neither of us speaking, the money on the table in front of us. The lights from the bars outside illuminate the metal table in front of us and somewhere there's the sound of glass shattering.

13.

When I get home there's a sign outside the front of the house—Greenbriar Realty—a picture of some nondescript white dude on the front, the phone number to call. I size up the sign and take in the green of the front lawn illuminated by the front porch, giant brown beetles hitting the ground with audible clicks and thumps as they careen toward the light.

Inside, the house becomes a mausoleum, all the furniture arranged in a particular kind of way and the marble countertops scrubbed and the pictures set into perfect places and the air perfectly cooled. Mom sits on the edge of one of the couches with a glass of white wine in her hand and the TV on mute and her eyes on her phone, a pair of sneakers on her feet and workout clothes but no sign of sweat. It's dark now and the house stands only illuminated by the candles on the edge of the kitchen counter and the black-white fuzz of the television set and the drum of the air conditioner running perpetually in the background.

"How'd it go?" she asks.

"Not well."

"Yeah?"

"I don't wanna talk about it."

"That bad?"

"Yeah. That bad."

"Sorry."

"What's the sign out front, Mom?"

She waves her hand around, pointing to the house, without taking her eyes off the phone.

"You can see."

"This all you?"

"Not all. Elise came over."

"I thought it was on the market September first."

"Didn't want to wait," she says.

"Are you sure, Ma?"

"More sure than I am about anything."

"Where will we go?"

"I don't know."

"Do you have a plan?"

"Do *you*?"

"I don't know. I just—"

"Do you want to stay?" she asks, suddenly pulling her eyes away from the phone. She looks at me with something in between sincerity and mild annoyance.

"In the house?"

"No. In Jersey. Anywhere near here."

"It's my senior year coming up."

"I know but . . . if you wanted to go. If you wanted to leave and go anywhere, I'd go with you."

"I don't want to go. I want to stay."

"I've got the money. Florida. California. Hawaii. Europe. Anywhere."

"This is where he lived. This is where he died too, Ma. I don't want to . . . Mom, I can't just give it all up in a month. I can't lose it all."

"We're not losing it all," she says, standing up, edging toward frantic. "We're not losing it all. We're grieving. We're using grief—we're moving forward. We—I can't stay like this. Declan, I need you to understand me. I can't stay in this house and see him around every corner. I can't make dinner at night and not hear him bounding down the stairs. There's—I tried to make myself a sandwich today, Dec. There's mustard in the fridge that he bought. Dijon mustard. I remember him specifically bringing it home. I can't even—his room still smells like those Marlboros. I can't be here anymore. Please, Declan. Let's go. Let's go anywhere."

I'm shaking my head, trying to look away.

"I just need something to stay consistent. I need something to stay. I need something to come home to," I say.

She walks up to me and puts both her hands on my shoulders.

"I do too. I do too, Declan. But it can't be here. It can't be here. You have to respect me on this one. You have to understand."

"And what? You're just supposed to ignore how I am feeling? I mean *fuck*."

"I'm not ignoring how you are feeling—"

"You are. You most definitely are. I've made it so clear. I need to stay. I need to stay here. I need the same school and the same friends and the same stupid parties. I've already lost the team, I've lost Chase . . . I lost this fucking song. I just need something to stay. Anything."

"I understand," she says, pulling her head down.

"No you don't. You don't understand."

"I do understand," she pleads.

"No you don't. You don't. You just fucking don't."

She pushes me back and away, violent.

"Fuck! Declan, I'm your mother. How much of myself have I put on hold for both of you? And I get *this—this* level of gratitude from one of you, and the other one goes and fucking kills himself. Yes I'm angry. I'm furious at him. I'm so angry. And I hurt. I am crying myself to sleep every night and I'm so angry and it hurts more than anything. And all of it—every corner I cut in my own heart, every aspiration I ever put on hold. For what? For fucking what?!"

The house is quiet now save for the sound of the air conditioner in the background, the flicker of the candles behind us, the nothing emanating from the TV. Mom stares at me with something between regret and hurt.

"I'm leaving tomorrow," she says softly, her eyes still locked on me. "LBI. Hell, maybe California. I don't know. Come with me. Don't come with me. Do whatever makes you happy. I can't protect you. I sure as hell couldn't protect him."

She turns back to the couch and sits down, pulls out her phone, starts scrolling again. I stare at her for a second and I don't know what I'm feeling or what to feel, much as it has been since he died. The TV flashes more silent stories of carnage and decadence. Everything inside of the moment seems so vacuum-sealed and tight and sad, choking in on itself.

"I see him, Mom, too. I talk to him too. Every day. You're not the only one."

I leave the room softly and head upstairs.

In my bed I check Chase's Snap location and peg him still in the same spot just a little south of Tampa. I watch the red dot flicker and think about sending him something but don't. I think of the moments where I could've called out to him or Mason or anybody and pivoted the course of life into the tiniest different direction, shifted the needle in the smallest direction.

I open the laptop and stare at the document untouched since the last time I opened the computer: *Leaning into the Dark*. I try to scribble a few words but nothing comes out and I slam the computer shut as hard as I can.

I read the unread messages from Lizzy she'd sent throughout the day—the breakfast sandwich she had, a bike ride on the boardwalk, a Dirty Heads concert she wants to go to in a couple of days, and a handful of selfies and messages scribbled with heart symbols.

I send The Ghost a message just as I'm falling asleep, as I start to drift into dreaming and everything blends into black and white and gray and the line between sleeping and waking blurs and I can hear the voices of the dead speaking themselves back into life.

You awake?

The DM sits for a second.

Yes.

What are you doing?

Nothing.

Mom's selling the house.

Yeah?

September 1st. Says she can't live in it without you.

Yeah she couldn't live with me in it either.

I sit back, unsure how to reply.

That's not true.

The dot-dot-dot lights up and then nothing and my eyes are flickering and fading. I wait for it. It doesn't come, it never comes, and then it all goes dark.

Mason comes to me in a dream that night. He stands quiet inside of a storm on the edge of the sand and he turns to face me with a smile on his face and motions for me to follow him and I walk toward him and get closer and closer, so close that I could touch him with my hands, reach out and pull out of the dream and into the world again but when I reach he fades and recedes, evaporating into the air in front of me. I am outside of my own body, staring at him as he dances along the water's edge, disintegrating slowly, and when I try to speak, it is just the silence of the dream and the night. He is dead and eternal and gone and alive, outside of time and space in a world where we can say hello again and ask for forgiveness and sit beside one another stripped of all the shattered hearts that defined our life.

"Mason, Mason . . . please come home."

These are the words that I try to say inside of the dream. I hear nothing. I feel nothing.

"I want to wake up, Mase. I want to wake up."

I repeat it again and again to myself but hear nothing. He turns to me at one point as if he can listen, and his face is ashen and grief-stricken as if the words landed like a barb in his side.

Sometime in the middle of the night I wake up. I'm staring at the ceiling trying to fall asleep again when I hear it: creaking and what sounds like soft shuffling in the distance. I listen more carefully and start to drift again when I hear the same floorboards creaking and the shuffling now louder.

I'm walking the hallways half-asleep trying to pinpoint the sound when I hear another creak and crack and something that sounds like movement and then I'm moving slowly down the stairs. Dudes will pack themselves into a car up in Newark and drive down to the beach downs, steal catalytic converters, and raid the cars sitting in the shiniest looking driveways.

But downstairs there's nothing, no sounds, just the same bleating of the air conditioner. I wander around the kitchen and the living room, check the basement and the closets and wander through the house as softly as I can. I listen for the creaking of the floorboards and the sound of feet shuffling but nothing.

On my way down the main hallway, I'm ready to turn up the stairs when I catch the glint of the light on the front of the door, lighting up the lock sitting in an unlocked position.

I don't sleep much after.

X

In the morning I try to find "Song for the Dead" on YouTube but it's already gone. I text Jake and ask him if he's heard from Price and he says he hasn't heard anything. I wander the house again before Mom wakes up and look for anything at all really but nothing's there and the house looks just as I left it when I went to sleep.

Jake replies after a bit.

I think we fucked up.

Downstairs, Mom stirs a spoon inside of her coffee mug and watches as I sit down across from her. Outside gray rain clouds sit high in the sky and the sun is blocked and the pelting of rain on the stained wood of our deck and the splish-splash of rain in our pool.

"When are you leaving?" I ask.

"I'll pack the car up. We can be out of here early in the morning. Should be back by Monday."

"Are they showing the house this weekend?"

"Yeah. It's in your interest to come with me. Otherwise you'll have to find somewhere to stay."

"Okay."

"I'm sorry about last night," she says.

"Me too."

"Will you come with?"

"What are we going to do?"

"I don't know. Not be here."

"For how long?"

"Just a few days. This house will fly off the shelves, I hope."

"I still can't believe we're leaving."

"Well, believe it. I'm sorry if I'm being callous. I really am. It just has to happen. For us. For the family."

"Family?" I offer, shaking my head.

"Yes," she says, leaning forward. "Family. Even us. A family."

A beat.

"Do you think they're going to find him?" I ask. "Find his body I mean."

"Probably not," she says. "And by this point . . . I don't even know what would be left."

"I dreamed about him again."

"Yeah?"

"I couldn't speak. He couldn't hear me."

"I see him every night, but I never can remember his face. I'm afraid of that—that there'll be a day where I can't even remember what he looked like."

"I don't think that'll ever happen."

"My grandmother—without a picture I couldn't. And every time I see a picture it's different than what I remember. Memory works in fragments. It pieces things together. Fills in the holes. Covers up the stuff that hurts. Forgets the stuff that really hurts. Right now—I remember the last fight Mason and I had. I wonder what would've been different if I'd said something different, done something different. But maybe there'll be a day where I don't remember it. Maybe that's the thing that hurts too much to hold onto."

"Where do you think he is?" I ask.

"Like now?"

"Yeah."

"What do you think?" she asks.

"I don't know. They—you hear it all about the next life. Somewhere else. Somewhere looking down. But it always sounds so stupid—eternity that is. I don't know."

"But what if you didn't know?" she asks. "What if you didn't know what eternity was? What if time was just . . . everywhere around you? What if you could be inside of every moment ever at the same time?"

She takes a sip of her coffee, stares at the rain outside.

"That's what I think when I think about Mason. I hope he is on the water by the jetty on thirteenth. I hope he's on the lawn at PNC. I hope he's swinging a baseball bat in a tee-ball league. I hope he is holding somebody's hand. I hope he is all of those things at the same time. I don't know what else to hope for. Maybe that I will see him again. Someday. In some form."

She turns back to me.

"That story you're writing. You still working on it?"

"I stared at it last night. Couldn't do much with it."

"Still stuck."

"I don't know what to write about with him dying. Once I start bullshitting it, it turns into bullshit. It just becomes something that it isn't. It feels false. It feels like I'm lying."

"Well," she says, "maybe the truth is too much for his story then. Maybe he deserves more than the truth. Something different or better."

A beat.

"How late were you up last night?" I ask.

"What do you mean?"

"I don't know. I woke up. Heard things."

"Your mind can play tricks."

A beat.

"I'm sorry all this happened."

"You don't have to apologize for anything. You don't have to be anything."

"I'm just sorry. That's all."

She shakes her head.

"So am I, Dec. So am I. But you're still here. I'm still here. Look at me. Look at me. We're still here."

14.

I MEET LIZZY AT THE WATERFRONT in Asbury Park, on the border of the boardwalk by the Pony, staring out at the Atlantic Ocean and whatever band had ambled its way onto the Summer Stage. Outside she kisses me and then she flashes an ID at one of the bouncers, some big burly Italian dude who just nods his head at both of us and puts a stamp on both of our wrists and lets us in.

Upstairs a gaggle of divorcees and newly single post-mid-life-crisis dads and a couple of out-of-place twenty-somethings standing around in awkward circles with fancy drinks in their hands looking alien and spaced. She points to two empty barstools at the bar and takes me there and we sit and she passes me her Vaporesso and I have a few pulls and then she takes it back. The bartender, a girl with blond hair and a tattoo on her shoulder that says *LOVE* comes over and does a double take before sighing and asking us what we're drinking and Lizzy orders two scotch and sodas on the rocks. The bartender gives us a long stare before shaking her head and heading toward the liquor.

We're quiet and the bartender brings the drinks with one of those floatie swords in each of them. She smiles a smile and pushes the drinks toward us, slopping some over the sides of both.

"Enjoy," she says.

A beat.

"Think she spit in them?" Lizzy asks.

"I had my eyes on her the whole time."

"You never know. They're pros by now."

"Who's the bouncer?" I ask, wrapping my fingers around the drink.

"Just some guy I know."

"Ex?"

"In a particular sense of the word—sure."

I take a sip.

"Never had one of these," I say.

"Yeah?"

"Jesus."

"They do the trick," she says.

"Yeah?"

"Get a pineapple juice on your way out. Pineapple juice always does the trick."

"I'll make note of it."

She raises her glass.

"A toast."

"To what?"

"I don't know. Being alive."

"To being alive," I say.

She clinks the glasses together and takes a sip. I follow, my eyes still on her.

"You still think this is a fling?" I ask.

"Ah, man, come on. That was a great toast."

"Sorry."

"And now you're apologizing. For what? Such a buzzkill."

"Alright, alright."

She puts her hand on mine.

"What do you want from this?" she asks.

"Us?"

"Yeah."

"I don't know really."

"Just tell me. You want to get married? You want to have kids? Run away? Come on. Tell me."

"I mean I don't know. I just . . . I think I like you."

"Yeah and?"

"I just . . . I don't know."

She smiles.

"Off in some other moment again," she says. "Look around. It's beautiful. Look at the view. The ocean in the distance. It's summer in New Jersey. You're alive. You're breathing."

"Yeah," I say, head down.

"Yeah what?"

"I don't know. I'm just all back and forth. I don't know what I'm feeling. I'm so fucking angry sometimes. And then there's nothing some days. And some days it hurts so bad. It's just—nothing is clicking. Nothing is working."

"And with me?"

"I mean, you're the one who doesn't want this to become anything serious."

"Just because it isn't serious doesn't mean it lacks some kind of worth. Come on. These will be memories you'll have forever."

"I guess."

She shakes her head.

"Maybe one day you'll look back and you'll tell your kid or your grandkid about the first girl you ever really liked.

Maybe you'll even use the word love. I'll be a part of your story. That's all it is. That's all it has to be."

She points to the balcony.

"Let's go for a walk," she says.

Outside warm August wind whips between us. The water comes in waves on the horizon, the sun a darker shade of orange as dusk moves in.

"This is good," I say, pointing to the drink.

"Yeah," she says, not turning her head.

"Do you think this will last forever? What I'm feeling?"

"About me?"

"No. About him."

She hesitates.

"I don't know if there's a playbook for these things," she says. "I don't know if people are supposed to know what to do. I think you just survive by trying. Taking a step forward or something like that. You can't do anything else. You can't just stop."

"You can though."

"How so?"

"You can just stop. There's these Facebook groups online. About grief. Somebody said it was like running a race. That everybody has their own pace, and some people stop moving for a while, or move more slowly. But that's not true.

Some people just don't start the race. Some people just stay stuck, not moving, the world passing them by."

"I guess then it's a choice."

"I don't buy that. You don't know what I'm feeling."

"Yeah, I don't. But at some point, it doesn't matter, right? At some point . . . who gives a shit?"

"What?" I say sharply.

"No listen to me. It—I mean, it happened. It's over. And now you have to do something. The something can be nothing, I guess. The something can be imploding. But it has to be something."

Her voice trails off at the end. I catch the neon light of the ceiling sparkling inside the teardrops forming in her eyes.

"You don't think I know about these things. You don't know everything, Declan."

"Are you alright?" I ask.

"Yeah, I'm fine. I'm fine."

"What's wrong?"

"It's hard to explain. It's nothing, I promise. I'll be fine."

She takes another sip of her drink.

"I'll be fine."

Ж

Outside later we go to the same place Chase and I had gone a few weeks prior, underneath the boardwalk close enough to the Pony that we can hear the music. She doesn't tell me why, but she cries for a while and she puts her head on my shoulder and I don't ask any questions. Then she just breathes and I listen to her breathing before she picks up her head and leans in. We make out for a while and she puts her hand inside my shirt and I put my hand inside of hers. We don't go much further than that and at some point we just lie back in the sand, our eyes on the Atlantic horizon now dark and blue in the fading sunlight. She says that she thinks August is the saddest of all the months and I ask her why and she says it's when you start to feel everything start to fade and leave, and she wonders if moments and memories and people are the same as months or days or years, moving into the past and receding into the dark and shifting and changing and how if you could, you could just reach out and catch a second or a picture frame or the smell of a joint moving through the air in the spring or the way a fire smells in October or how snowflakes look melting into brown asphalt, a moment inside the palm of your hand.

"But you can't," she says. "They just vanish. Behind us. Vanish forever. And one day you'll vanish too. Like everything. Gone. Just a memory."

"You don't know that," I say.

"But I do. And you do too. We're young. We're inside of a dream we'll be having for the rest of our lives. We're inside of a memory. And you only chase those things, right, because you never find them again."

"You think too much," I say.

"That's rich coming from you," she says.

She leans back into me and I lean into her, the music pouring in from the stage, a band I don't even recognize, slinking guitar solos and the snap of snare drums and the thump of the bass drum. For a while we drift into one another quietly and it feels like one of those moments she's talking about, even if I can feel the edges of her slipping away, receding backwards, soon to be out of reach.

Later it's different—the sound of frantic voices and panicked shouts, both of us sitting on the benches on the boardwalk now, watching the stories she'd started getting texts about. We pull closer to each other when the video starts with labels like *UNCENSORED* and *GRAPHIC 18+*. The video is clear and easy to see, a man standing beside the edge of a building, a government building, we catch a glimpse of a small crowd forming around a man near the edge of where he stands. He's waving something in his hand and shouting and there are people shouting back at him and for a second I wonder if it's a bomb or a gun and I can feel my heart moving into my throat but then I see the wetness soaked into his hair and the way his t-shirt is hanging off of his body and I hear the words "no" and "please don't do this" come like fractures out of the phone and it's only then that I catch the glint of the silver from the lighter in his hand, and at the second I know what it is, there's a flash and a flicker and the entire frame of the man is engulfed in flames almost instantly. The crowd around him backs up and I hear screams—panicked, horrified screams—muted slightly by the quality of the phone's audio. Lizzy pulls herself closer to me when she watches and behind those screams, ever so quickly, the shouted groans and intermittent shrieks of the man as he burns alive in front of us.

LIBERATE US. LIBERATE YOURSELVES.

—the message they find later on his Facebook

I drop Lizzy off later in the night. I watch her walk to the front door and open it and I try to peer inside to get some picture of what her life is like outside of her time with me but no hand opens the door and all the lights are off and even when I pull away a little bit and drive down the road far enough that she can't see me but I can still see the house I catch no glimpses of anything, just a hallway light coming on and coming off and then the house sitting in the dark.

I drive to the Manasquan Bridge again and pull over about a half mile before and walk my way up the bridge toward its center. I put my hands and head over the edge and stare down at the water and imagine falling.

Where are you now?

I wait for the message to go through, the service dim on the top of the bridge, and when it clears I watch the message appear inside of the DMs and then watch the dot-dot-dot light up again and come and go and come and go.

Where are you?

The Ghost asks.

Where you died

Where you think I died

Meet me where we learned to surf. Prove it to me. Prove to me you're him and that you're alive.

The dot-dot-dot lights up again and again and then another message.

Soon.

Then you're just a scammer. Just like I know you are. Prove it to me now. I want it now. Not later. Now.

No response.

I drive down to the spot, where Ocean Avenue and Sixteenth collide, and sit on the brown polished wood of the boardwalk, my feet hanging off the edge, the sand beneath me. There's water moving in the distance as there always is. I imagine closing my eyes and dialing myself backwards in time. I imagine a wave cresting over my head, my brother's hand on my back as he pushed me both away from it and toward what it had to teach me.

I'm here

I sit and watch the message go through and wait for the response but none comes.

Later that night, I wander through the dark of my house and put my hands on the walls and listen to the sounds of the air moving and the humming swirl of the dishwasher and catch the smell of old white wine in a glass that hasn't been washed and a cigarette ashed inside of a tumbler outside and crickets humming by the pool, and I sit outside listening to the night and waiting for The Ghost to come and walk into the house again but nothing comes and nobody visits and at some point I go upstairs and lay my head on the pillow and stare at the ceiling and imagine the sound of voices in the black.

ꟿ

The next morning, Mom wakes me up early and says she wants me to see something. She says to come downstairs and I say I will soon. I check my phone for messages from

The Ghost but nothing. I text Jake and ask him if he's heard anything or if he thinks he's going to hear anything. Then I'm scanning his Instagram and watching his old videos from the summer before.

I'm downstairs sipping from a cup of coffee and nibbling on an Eggo watching the news with Mom, evidently what she wanted to show me, and the newscasters look solemn and serious intoning whatever it is they're intoning.

LIBERATE US. LIBERATE YOURSELVES.

We listen. The burning man on the edge of the boardwalk isn't the only one—random coordinated immolations across the country, some kind of protest, or warning.

LABOR DAY WEEKEND

SEVEN DAYS

They flash more images of the tubes from weeks before, the devices that they're now referring to as explicitly nuclear, and the organizational pattern and coordination of the suicides suggesting that there's more heft and weight to the threats than anybody deemed previously. They say that the government has elevated the terror threat to red and that they expect violence to continue.

"I don't understand," I say.

Mom turns to me.

"Neither do I."

For a while we are quiet. The story gets grimmer. The news rings on about the immigration crisis and infection and disease and the end of all things American and the new threats The Liberators have been offering, suitcase nukes and small towns wiped off the face of the earth, and on one screen a man with a blue suit and red beady-eyed Rivers Cuomo glasses saying that the end had been sowed years ago in smallpox blankets and ground-up glass in biscuits and water, and on the next screen a woman with a white pantsuit and a blue pin in her hair saying that The Liberators had no affiliation with any political party whatsoever, and we disavow them, and all Americans should disavow them, but have we thought about what they're trying to say to us and how The Liberators wouldn't have ever come to be if somebody hadn't voted for somebody and somebody hadn't protested somebody else and someone hadn't said X or Y and how on the southern portions of the country there are waves of families and children wandering the desert, caked in dust and parched from dehydration, The Lost, boys and girls who had come across the border by themselves or had been separated from family and now were just wandering, homeless, without any anchor of any sort, and the uptick in the deaths and abandonment and misplacement of these children, many of whom were murdered by the ever-increasing gangs of anarcho-sympathizers or factions of random murders or aggressors or the decay and rot sluicing down the drain of the collective conscious or those same wandering Lost Boys and Lost Girls who'd declined into drugs and alcohol or were sold off into the sex trade or simply just vanished off the earth, swallowed up like plankton, receded into the faded background of the country, relegated to the textbooks that nobody would ever read, stories that nobody would tell, sung in the songs whose words nobody remembered, in the tales nobody wanted to say, relegated to wander the night as ghouls and ghosts surrounded by the hordes of people who just wanted them forgotten. The Liberators had promised to "save" the lost ones, and rumors spread that so many of them had joined the ranks of that shadow cult, looking for work or salvation or hope or even just a place to sleep, joining the ever-increasing number of American boys and girls who had just vanished into the night.

The Liberators were everywhere: splattered on posters and Instagram stories and TikTok accounts, their premonitions about the end of the world seemingly growing and growing, and how easy you could tell the sickness was spread, how the late-night Colbert jokes got less and less funny, ominous warnings about nigh judgment floating on pieces of scrap paper moving like embers beside abandoned cigarette boxes in deserted streets.

What do we do now?

What is coming?

What is the countdown moving toward?

"Mom," I say.

"Yeah."

"You ever see anything like this?"

She shakes her head.

"I don't think so. Maybe the towers. The same kind of feeling."

A beat.

"Are you still going?" I ask.

"Where?" she says.

"You said you were going away for a while."

"Only if you're coming with me," she says.

"I'm not coming with you. I don't want to go anywhere."

"Okay."

"Mom."

"Yeah."

"Can I tell you something?"

"Yeah."

"It's not gonna sound . . . I don't know."

"Okay . . ." she says hesitantly.

"I've been talking to somebody online. It started like an accident. I think . . . I thought . . . and I guess I still think it's a scam. But it's this account that . . . it says that it's Mason."

"What?"

"It's an account with his name. He's been talking to me since a few days after Mason died."

"Declan—"

"No, just listen. It says that it's him. It knows things that it shouldn't know. It knows conversations that I had with Mason, arguments, even talks we had the night he died . . ."

"Declan . . ."

"I don't know what to do. I don't know what even to think. They never found his body, right? What if he went into hiding? What if he just ran away? He's fucked up. He was always fucked up. Maybe he just made some kind of a mistake . . ."

"He did make some kind of a mistake, Declan. The worst kind of mistake."

"No, just listen."

"There's nothing to listen to, Dec," she says. Her voice is quiet. "Look what everything is doing to you. This crap on the television. Your brother. It's eating you from the inside out. Look at yourself."

"But what if it was? What if I can prove it?"

"Declan please—"

"Please, Mom. If it's him. I can prove it. I can prove that he's still alive. He knows . . . he knows things. And he says he wants to meet. Maybe it is him. And the other night, somebody was here, I think. I heard something . . ."

"Declan, listen to yourself."

"I know."

"No. Really listen to yourself."

"I know it sounds crazy."

"It sounds crazy Declan, because it is crazy. Your brother is dead. He died. It's been three weeks now. You're not speaking to him. You're talking to a bot, or a scammer, or a liar. Declan, please."

I'm looking away, shaking my head.

"It— He knows things that only Mason knew. Conversations only he and I knew about. Stories. It has to be him."

Mom stands up and comes close to me, puts her hands out and touches my face like I am a child.

"It's okay," she says.

"Mom please . . ."

"It's okay," she says, even more quietly than before, softer than I've heard her maybe ever.

"Stop saying it's okay. Just listen. Please just listen."

"Declan, there's nothing to listen to. It isn't real. He's dead. He's gone."

"There's no body, Mom."

She shakes her head. "I know."

"Then how can you be sure?" I say softly.

I let it hang in the air and I'm just staring at the reflection of the light inside of the coffee. She turns the TV off and then without saying anything she leaves me in the living room. For a second, I stay there in the silence but then it's all too loud, so I turn the television back on and the people on the screen start blaring about a heat wave on the East Coast and melting ice caps and polar bears starving. I turn the volume up as loud as I can, drown in it all. I scan Twitter for the worst stuff I can find, I want the worst since he died—I want to see and feel the worst. I watch it all. When it gets worse, I watch it again.

Later I'm wandering around the house looking for something to do so I roll a joint and smoke a little bit of it and that gets boring too and then I'm walking down the stairs to answer a doorbell, some UPS man or something, and when I open the door there's a face in front of me with a blank expression resting.

"Hey," Chase says, his eyes on me.

15.

WE'RE OUT IN THE BACKYARD sitting across from one another on the right side of the pool. The sun is beating down on both of us and we both have sunglasses on and both of us are sitting reclined in a chair with our legs splayed out in front of us.

"Who is she?" he asks.

"This girl I met."

"You like her?"

"I think so. I don't know."

He sips from a Poland Springs bottle that he's been holding.

"You still training?" I ask.

"Taylor let me back on the team. He texted me while I was in Tampa. Said we can't do without both of us."

"I won't be back."

"I figured."

"You doing anything?" he asks.

"Like what?"

"I don't know. All the free time you have now. Figured you'd be doing something."

"Nothing."

"Okay."

He finishes the bottle of water. He points to my foot.

"No more boot?"

"Fuck that," I say.

A beat.

"Dad says I can't see you," he says. "He says it's a phase. That I probably learned it in school. Stuff like that."

"Dude, I don't want to talk about it anymore."

"Okay."

I feel something like regret so I sit up.

"I'm sorry, I just—there's just a lot going on."

"Yeah," he says. "I know."

"It's not just Mason. I mean it is but—"

"The girl too . . ."

"Yeah, a little of that."

"What else?"

"I don't know. I sound like a crazy person."

"What do you mean?"

"It's nothing. It's just stupid."

"What's stupid?"

"I'm gonna sound like I'm losing my mind. I just—I've been talking to this thing online. An account. It says it's Mason. Sounds just like him. Talks just like him. Knows things about him that happened between us. And . . . it's driving me fucking crazy."

"Yeah?" Chase says with a level of sincerity.

"Yeah, I mean. Wait you believe me?"

"I mean you say you're talking to somebody. I believe that."

"Okay well . . . I don't know. It started a few days after he died. It's just like him. And. . . ."

"They never found him," Chase says.

"Never."

"So, you think it's actually him."

"I don't know. I mean no. But yes. I don't know."

"You want to believe it's him."

"Yeah," I say quietly. "Yeah I do."

"I get that," he says.

"And it's probably a scammer. Probably some fucking lunatic. But what if it isn't? What if he ran away? He was all over the place. You know that. I know that. And what if he just snapped and ran away? Down to Cape May. Delaware. Florida. I don't know. And he's just by himself somewhere hiding."

"Wouldn't there be some traces?"

"Like what?"

"I mean, did he have his own debit card? Credit card?"

"Yeah . . ."

"Wouldn't charges be popping up?"

"No," I say, gaining more confidence. "He thought . . . he thought every time you swiped or checked in it was some weird thing—the government tracking you."

"Ask him again."

"To meet?"

"Same spot. Ask him again. Call the bluff."

"It's not him," I say, trying to reassure myself.

"I mean . . . where's the body? Don't you think it would've washed up by now?"

"Currents maybe. I don't know."

"It's a river," he says. "Not the ocean. Where would he have drifted to?"

"I don't know."

"Call his bluff. Do it."

I sit further back in the chair. "Are you still pissed at me?" I ask.

"Not really."

"I don't even know what happened."

"Wild summer, right?" he asks.

"Yeah, I mean, but . . ."

"But what?"

"Are you?"

"I think so," he says. "Are you?"

I shake my head. "I don't think so. I don't know."

"Okay," he says.

"It's just been a fucked up summer—really fucked up."

"Yeah," he says, shaking his head and looking off at the pool. "Fucked up."

We're at Sixteenth and Ocean an hour later, sitting on the benches. I'm smoking a cigarette and Chase is drinking another bottle of Poland Springs. The messages we've sent to the *@mase_314* account have yet to be read. The sun is bright and beating, the heat blistering.

I'm at 16th and Ocean—where we learned to surf.

Meet me here.

If it's really you, come home. We've missed you.

It's time to come home.

A couple of bennies walk by loudly complaining about the beach badges they've paid for. A few midday joggers. A junkie rubbing his nose and scratching at his arms. We're looking at the people around us, the beach, the town, the planes flying by advertising drink specials at the Osprey and erectile dysfunction pills and voting rights.

"Feels weird, right? The state of things," Chase says.

"Yeah I guess."

"You remember history class freshman year? With Mr. Brown?"

"Yeah."

"You remember what he said? I think it was about the end of the Roman Empire. How that . . . during its peak they'd stage these fights at the Colosseum. Really spectacular shit. Gladiators. Naval battles. Wild stuff. But at the end there was none of it. They'd take homeless people. Men, women, children. Chain them up in the center of the sand and they'd just let hyenas and tigers run loose, eat them alive."

"Yeah, I remember that."

"I don't know why. It just stuck with me," Chase says, biting his thumbnail, looking around.

The phone buzzes.

When it's just you.

That's when I'll come.

I show Chase the message.

"How does he know?" Chase asks.

"He doesn't know. He's making it up. It's a bluff, like you said."

"Yeah maybe," Chase offers.

I type out a reply.

I am alone. Right now.

The dot-dot-dot lights up.

Chase is sitting next to you. I'm watching.

Everything goes quiet and vacuum-sealed for a moment and we both look around at the sea of people on the beach, on the boardwalk, sitting on their front porches, walking through the vines and orchids by the archway marking the entrance to Spring Lake. Every set of eyes that I lock on for even a second—Mason appears inside of each face for a flash, as if he has been gone for years and could've transformed into anyone. I stand up from the bench and walk a few steps, up the boardwalk closer to where we live, like I'm being called. I look out into the crowd for anyone, any shape that could be him, any semblance of his visage.

"I don't like this," Chase says from behind me, called out like a warning.

I turn around and make my way back to the bench. I shoot more messages back at the account.

You have to prove that you're him.

Really prove it.

I want a picture of you now. Not from weeks ago. Not as a kid. Now.

"It's bullshit," I say, still reassuring myself.

"I know. You're right."

The dot-dot-dot lights up quickly.

Why?

Because I'm stopping this now if it isn't you. I need to know you're alive.

I need to know.

There is a pause and a breath. When I was a sophomore—swapping nudes with this girl I'd met at the beach. The same kind of feeling. The dot-dot-dot lights up and sits there for a while, long enough that Chase starts to peer over my right shoulder as if he's trying to see what it is.

Then there's a picture.

Mason standing on the edge of the ocean, in the dark.

His face unshaven now, the shadow moving over his cheeks and his neck.

His eyes tired and glassy.

A dead cigarette hanging from his lips.

Dead.

But he's alive.

Inside of the picture, inside of the world maybe—he's alive.

I tell Chase I have to go and he asks if he can come with and I tell him to go home. He rides off back away from the water and for a few seconds I watch him vanish into the blue siding and asphalt sidewalks.

I ride my bike back home through the same sea of spectators and with each passing person I imagine inside them, behind them, underneath their floorboards, hiding in their basements, sleeping inside the motel adjacent to their home—Mason. I ride faster than I can remember riding down Ocean Avenue and the wind whips in my face warm and humid and hot, the humidity from the summer now relentless and unceasing and the oxygen all but sapped out.

The air is warm and wet and the smell of hot dogs and grilled sausages on the air. I can hear the sound of Springsteen billowing out of somebody's car but none of it feels pastiche or wholesome, it all funnels into the same dull drone—

Where is he?

Where did he go?

Is he still alive?

Why hasn't he come home?

Inside of the house I'm moving towards Mom frantic, her legs propped up on the ottoman and a sweating glass of white wine in her hand, flowing robes on, now my arms outstretched and my mouth moving before I even know what's coming out. I hear her say something to me, some kind of question, and I can barely make out the words I'm now shouting at my mother.

"He's alive, Mom. He's alive."

"What?"

"I told you. He's alive. He sent me a picture today. It's him. It's definitely him."

I hold out my phone and hand it to her.

"Look," I say. "Look at him."

She picks up the phone and holds it in her hand and studies it for a second.

"Declan we have videos. The police have videos."

"Of a boy jumping. A boy. Not Mason. Another boy."

"Which boy, Declan? Who else has gone missing?"

"Kids are . . . think of how many kids have died around here the last few years. Think of the suicides and the drugs and the booze and all the things that kill everybody around here. It's so impossible that we haven't heard of one?"

"Declan, they showed me the video."

"Of him jumping?"

"No . . . it was him walking up the bridge. They zoomed in on his face. It was clearly him."

"So you never saw him jumping?"

"Declan, Jesus Christ. He's dead. You have to let it go."

"Maybe I'm wrong," I say. "Sure. Maybe. But what if I'm not? Don't you want to see him again? Don't you want to see him alive again—inside of this house?"

She closes her eyes, puts her hand on the bridge of her nose.

"Declan, I want all of those things more than anything. Don't you understand?"

"Mom . . ."

She takes another look at the phone. Something about it seems even to break her.

"It does look like him. I'll give you that. But Declan think . . . clearly and rationally. Just think," she says.

"I know, Mom. I wouldn't have brought it if it didn't."

She slaps herself in the face gently. "I have to wake up. I've got to sober up. We can—I mean, we can just go to where that picture is. Where is that picture? Do you know? That could clear it up. Maybe that."

"I don't know. I didn't recognize it."

"He's gone, Declan. You know that, right? He's gone. I'll check with you. We'll figure it out. But he's gone."

She shuffles around for a second, fumbles for the keys on the counter, puts them down, and walks away. Behind me, I hear her heading up the stairs.

I'm still here

The Ghost screams from inside the phone.

Lizzy texts and says that she's around the corner, and when I'm opening the front door she's already there, her hair wet from the ocean and her skin tan and her face lit up by the sun that now sets earlier in August.

"You want to roll?" she says.

"Not tonight," I say.

"You got better plans?" she smiles.

"No I just—sorry, I can't tonight."

"Are you alright?"

"Yeah, I'm fine. I just can't. I have to go somewhere."

"Okay," she answers, shrugging.

She walks the bike up the driveway and leans it into the side of the house.

"Something I said?" she asks.

"No. No, I promise."

She smiles.

"We can ride underneath the boards again. Sneak into your bedroom after dark. There's only so many days left in the summer."

"No," I say, more firmly. "Not tonight."

A beat.

"Okay," she says. "Then I'm out of your hair."

"Okay," I say, sitting on the front stoop.

"Are you sure you're okay?"

"I'm fine," I say.

"Do you want to talk?" she asks.

"Fucking A. No. I don't want to talk. I just—please just go. It's not personal. Please just go."

For the first time, something like anger moves through her eyes. She sighs, kicks the brakes off the bike, and sits back down. Without a word she pedals down the driveway, into the street, out of sight.

I'm scrolling through my phone and tapping my foot on the concrete. An ice cream truck sounds in the distance and I hear kids shouting.

I scroll through Mason's account—the real Mason. I look at some pictures from a party a year before. I find his graduation shots with Jake from high school. The comments littered below. I find the few straggling comments from the well-wishers wishing him back to life. Every picture on his page is the same and has been since he died—random friends, acquaintances, occasional strangers, woken up in the middle of the night with some vision of him hurtling toward his doom and wondering what they could have done to set the axis right again.

And then I'm on my bike again—cutting through the August air.

Jake's mom is on the front steps of their porch when I get there. She has her hair clipped up, a lime-green robe on, furry sandals, a litany of gold and silver bracelets. She lets the cigarette in her mouth drop when she sees me park in front of her house, walk up the stoop to the door.

"Here for Jake?" she asks.

I don't answer. Jake opens the door before I can reach for the doorknob and he smiles and motions for me to come in, but I don't, I just stand there for a second, fire rising, before swinging as hard as I can at his face. There's an audible crack and he pulls himself back, nearly falls to the floor. I watch as he thuds onto the hardwood and nearly cracks his head behind him.

"It's you, right?" I shout, stepping closer to him.

"What the fuck . . . ?" he mumbles underneath his breath, blood now seeping between clenched fingers over his nose.

"It's you. Only you could know shit like that. Only you."

"Fucking A, man. Jesus Christ."

"It's you. Admit it's you. Just tell me. Tell me it's you."

He stands up, pulling his bloodied hand back. I don't move. He cocks his fist back for a moment, a longer moment, and then pulls it down.

"I'm not throwing a punch," he says.

I watch his eyes move behind me and I turn. His mother stands there, the cigarette now in her hand. For a moment I'm trying some mania on her face, but I don't see it. She's calm. Deadly calm. I turn back to Jake. He pulls his hand away, whips some of the blood onto the floor.

"He's gone Dec. Gone," he says.

"Show me your phone."

"What?"

"Show me your fucking phone."

He wipes more blood from his face before reaching into his pocket, pulling out his phone, and handing it to me. He tells me the password and then I'm inside of it, scrolling through his Instagram. I click around—look for another account. There's nothing.

"You're coming apart," he says.

"I'm not," I say, more softly than I intended. "I'm not."

"Mason is dead," he says. "Gone."

I shake my head.

"You don't know that."

He spits more blood onto the floor.

"Then go find him," he says. "Prove it."

He stares at me, the setting sun inside of his eyes. I turn to face his mother, the ash from the cigarette now limp and hanging from the cigarette's end.

"Still chasing a ghost," she says.

I'm parked about a half mile from their house, minutes later, screaming and punching the roof of the car.

I am inside of the warehouse where we used to practice. I am standing on the bridge where they told me he died. I am inside of the school that he grew up in, and I am standing on the front yard where we used to throw a baseball. I am at the bar on the edge of the Manasquan River where he still orders the fish and chips inside of my dreams, and I am standing on the edge of Spring Lake with a freshwater rod in the water, my brother's hand outstretched to the lily pads on the edge of the crisp autumn water.

I am driving through town, wordlessly and silently at first, looking on every street corner, down every alleyway, at the stoop of every mom-and-pop liquor store and at the entrance to the Pony and inside of broken carnival rides, at the bottom of a Ferris wheel that doesn't spin, at a snack bar with a silver gate pulled down in front of it.

"Where is he, Mom? Where is he?"

This is how we spoke on the night you died. This is how we speak today.

The Ghost doesn't reply. The night comes. I hit refresh on his page a million times, waiting for a new follower or an unfollowed account or a new message or a picture of anything. Nothing changes. The algorithm evolves and becomes more and more demented with each pull of my finger, sniper videos from the Gaza Strip and children being beheaded and a piece of jackfruit rotting in the open jungle and a tsunami washing a village away. I feel myself tethered to the madness and the insanity and every time I want to quit, pull the plug, throw the phone away and delete the account and move back into the world, I just drift further and further into the dark.

I need you to answer me

Fucking answer me

That's a real picture, isn't it?

You're alive.

You made us go through all that and you're alive.

Answer me.

Come back.

Come back to me.

I fall asleep on the couch that night, the TV on, my phone resting on my knee. The front door is unlocked. I know, because I was the one who unlocked it.

Ж

Mom spends the next day at the police station—says she is reporting a missing person. When they try to explain to her that the missing person is dead, she shows them the screenshot of the pic the account sent me.

Do you see? she says.

This is my son. Do you see?

The day moves the same as the day before it. Underneath bridges, wandering through trails in Thompson Park, standing on the bridge into Sea Girt and watching the cars pass. I bike down to Point Pleasant, down to the boardwalk, and for minutes I'm standing in the center of the boardwalk, the masses moving around me.

That night I throw on a light t-shirt and wander into downtown, past Anchor Tavern and Boathouse and the hardware store and the occasional straggler wandering down the street stops when I pull out the picture and put it close, uncomfortably close, to any face that walks by.

"This is my brother. Mason. Have you seen him?"

"This is my brother, Mason. He's missing. He's been missing for a while—he's alive. He's alive I know it. Do you know where he is? Do you recognize him at all?"

"This is my brother, Mason."

"This is my best friend Mason. He's gone. Have you seen him?"

Summer rain starts to fall. The sound of faint footsteps on wet asphalt. I am still wandering inside of the dark. Softly a summer storm moves upon the town and the wanderers and vagabonds and townies leave the streets. For a moment in the dark, in the storm, you can look down the street and see what the winters around here become: the emptiness and the cold and the gray and the wet, the haze that hangs over the town when the town is put to sleep.

Most of the faces I see don't recognize him. Some of them remember the story from a few weeks prior or they knew somebody else who died or somebody's cousin or anything like that, but none of them talk about seeing him today, in a moment, at a grocery store or wandering the streets or anything like that.

"You'll find him soon," one old lady says, her eyes wet and her skin like paper.

And what does that mean? Soon? And where? Where can I find him? Inside of my head now—inside of my memory. Is there anywhere else now?

Before I head home, I drive up and down Ocean Avenue, passing through the towns quietly, watching the rain make patterns on the windshield. I put on the quietest music I can find and let it all take me in—a feeling of blue, a feeling of scraping and tearing and numbness that feels like it may last forever. When the night gets long enough and the sky dark enough, I find myself back at the spot where I asked The Ghost to meet, the junction where Mason and I learned to surf. I stare out at the dark of the sea and listen to the sound of the waves crashing into themselves and the splashing of the rain on the wood beneath me. Time moves like light in September—fading and fleeting and moving into the cold, and I wonder about the moments that I had with him that I lost in the same way—peanut butter sandwiches. I hear the voices inside me telling me that I'm stuck, that I cannot move on, and that I have to move on, but that is the truth: that I am stuck, and that there is no moving on from this kind of loss.

When I sleep that night, I'm at home as a boy, playing Mortal Kombat, my brother trying to teach me one of Scorpion's fatalities, and then the dream breaks apart into spider webs of broken glass and somebody comes to see me inside the dream, a faceless boy standing alone in an empty room, a figure I've been chasing since I can remember.

I meet Lizzy at her house the next night, outside her front door, the grass overgrown now on the front lawn, some of the bushes and trees in the front yard brown and scorched from the heat of the summer. The sun is setting, and it lights up the yard yellow and orange. I am at the front door knocking when it opens and she is standing in front of me.

"Sorry," I say.

She turns, steps out of the house, and shuts the door behind her.

"I don't like you here at the house," she says. "I'd rather meet somewhere."

"Sorry," I say.

She runs her hands through her hair.

"Why are you here?" she asks.

"I didn't know what to do. I don't know who to talk to."

"Declan, I want to be there for you. I really do."

"But what?"

She offers a faint smile, dangling some kind of sadness from the corners of her lips.

"This is a fling, Declan. And . . . things don't last forever with me."

"Fuck. Not this again. Please."

"It's just not that. Maybe I would want to try. But you're . . . tethered to this thing. And I know that sounds selfish and I cannot even imagine what you are feeling or thinking. But I can't be tethered too."

"Fuck," I whisper.

"It's not that I don't care. Maybe I love you. Maybe you love me. I don't know. But this isn't going to last. It's not supposed to last."

"Today of all days . . . *this* is the day you tell me?"

"The summer is coming to an end. This will too. You didn't know me before. You won't know me after. You know why I move around. I know at least. It was fun while it lasted. And it doesn't change anything about it. It's just . . . done soon. Maybe sooner rather than later."

I'm desperate, on the verge of tears.

"So what is it then? What's next?" I ask.

"I want to show you something," she says, pulling my hand and leading me back into the car. Inside she hands me her phone with the black screen of a preloaded video already up on it.

"Listen to me," she says. "I want you to hit play on this. And I think it might hurt you. It might make you furious. But I want you to hit play. And don't judge me please. Just wait till the end."

I push the phone down onto my leg and rest it before pressing the horizontal triangle and waiting. In a moment, Mason is standing in front of me, wedged inside of the screen. He's standing inside of a room, a nondescript room, nothing I recognize. His face is there, just as it was the day he left. He smiles the same smile at me. His eyes are the same blue.

"Hey, buddy," he says.

"What is this?" I ask.

"Just wait . . . just listen," she says, pointing back to the screen.

"You want me to be alive. You want me to be somewhere besides where I am. Most of the days you're awake—that's all you can imagine. That I'll walk in the front door, bring home a pizza for dinner, or whatever. But I won't, because I'm not here anymore. I'm dead. I will be dead forever. You won't find me anywhere, on any boardwalk, inside of any cellphone. I am gone."

Inside of the video he stares at me with the same expression as he started. The room hasn't shifted. His face is Mason's—but something about it is missing. There's some quality, some warmth, some light that isn't in his eyes. This is my brother alive, approximated.

"There are so many programs out there now, Dec," she says. "They're everywhere. I took one of the photos you have on your Instagram. I put it through some filters. I gave it a background. And then I gave it a script. This is pretty good now. Think of how good it'll be in a couple of months, even years. Politicians can give speeches that they've never written or spoken. I can present on something that I know nothing about. Hell—even the fucking Liberators, who knows, right? How much of it is real? Maybe these people we see on television were made from photographs. Maybe they don't exist. Maybe The Liberators don't exist. Anything can be anything—reality can be shifted into whatever we want it to be. And the dead can never die."

"Why did you do this?" I ask.

"Because you need to let him go," she says. "Mason is gone. Your brother is gone."

"No I mean . . . I know, but . . . maybe there's—"

"No," she says, putting her hand pointedly on mine. "There's nothing. It's over. He's gone."

"They never found his body," I say.

"Maybe they never will."

"So what was the point?" I ask.

"Of what?" she says.

"The texts. If they're not him. What are they trying to get at?"

"Does it matter? A scammer—the same way they tell old people to bail out their grandson from jail. Or some stupid fucker just getting his rocks off. That shitty kid on the team you told me about. Who gives a shit? It's not real."

"That's just what you believe," I say weakly.

"No. It's what you know too."

She pulls the video away from me and I reach for the image like I am reaching for him. I hold my hand out and wait but she pulls the phone all the way back.

"Can I watch more?" I ask.

"Why?"

"It's him," I say. "It's still him."

She puts the phone in her pocket and leans toward me. She kisses me on the cheek and pulls me closer and then she is embracing me. She holds on tight, and for a moment I resist, but then it feels like warmth and peace and I find myself falling into her.

"It isn't. And it never was."

We stay inside of the car like this for what feels like minutes. Outside there is the din of thunder and the rain starts to fall, splashing down the windowpanes, accenting the quietness of our breathing inside the car, both of us not speaking.

I will be at the Sixteenth Ave entrance tonight—
the place where we used to surf. 6p.m.
Right down the street from where we live.
You can find me there, Mason.
You can find me there.
And if there's somebody else listening, that's
where you can find me too.
One for one.
Please just let him go.
Take me.
Please.

I leave Lizzy's house and I am sitting in the car adjacent to the boardwalk right before six. Another storm picks up on the ride over. I drive through it, through the gray and the splash of August rain, through red lights and the haze in my eyes, through the quiet breathing of The Ghost inside of my mind, inside my heart.

On the boardwalk, the sound of water and the splash of car tires in the distance. The bars and shops lining Ocean Avenue still lit with the dwindling daylight and all the hooligans that accompany its end. The pizza joints, the ice cream shops approaching their close. The beam of headlights and the cavalcade of memories.

I am standing in the rain, soaked to the bone. I am staring out at the ocean and watching the green and blue crash into white. In the cold and in the dark I see my life over the next days, weeks, months, years . . . decades. A string of pearls pulled out over the horizon, stretched into tapestry. What else is there besides grief now? What else can come from this?

I see myself at home: a frozen pizza dinner and old movies, Mom asking me where I've been and me not having the heart to tell her. She falls asleep alone that night and I put her to bed when the storms roll in. When she's out, I wander through the house and listen for the voices of the dead. I fall asleep on the couch, freefall into bad dreams again. I see the cycle beginning. The sound of the ocean. Wind whipping down the boards. Nobody comes. And then the nights come, groundhog days, the endless repetition: the same message on the same social handles, the same pleas, the same questions, where did you go, where are you now, when are you coming home . . . time passing. More frozen dinners. More old movies and more putting Mom to bed when she falls asleep or gets cold or hears a sound late at night. More lonely echoes inside an empty house. Every night after he doesn't show, I put up the same message.

I will wait for you. Forever.

I wait for my brother on that boardwalk, I wait for a ghost. I wait for the black and the dark.

The empty nights, the reruns, the recycled news stories, the soft plop of cold rain, the reverb inside of a broken home, the whisper of snow on the pavement. I take trips to nowhere, hunches and gut instincts, bars where somebody knows one thing or somebody else knows another thing, police stations where they keep records on all the ones who've left or vanished, and at night, I come home and drive to the same place every time, park in the same spot two spaces away from the boardwalk stairs, the spot where he and I, in some memory far away now, were boys once, toes in the sand, eyes on the horizon, waiting to grow up and grow old, to tell the stories of how we were to our kids, how those stories never came, now those stories folded into an elegy, a refrain that lasts till time breathes its final breath.

"Where is he? Where is my son?" she asks sometimes.

"I'm going to find him, Mom. I promise. I will bring him home."

But time passes. Winter turns to spring. Spring turns to summer. I wait and wait for the messages I put up every night to bring some reckoning for Mason, but the waiting is all.

I see streaks of gray and stubble creep onto my face. I see the calls, the voicemails, the texts that I send to Lizzy, years later. She is holding someone's hand underneath a pine tree, she is guiding a child's feet on hardwood floors, she is letting snow melt in calloused hands in water. She says that if I look harder, I will find more stories to tell, and that maybe finding Mason is impossible—but speaking about him, talking about him, bringing him out of memory is the only thing that we can do with the dead once they have gone.

I see myself in the future, with someone at my side, their face warm, my hands cold. She asks me if I can let him go, that she'll stay with me if I can walk into tomorrow with her, without him. I tell her that I can't, that his ghost, and all the ghosts, have to come with us, together. I beg her to stay—I say that I can move into tomorrow, but not alone. *What if you never find what you're looking for*?

I watch lines slide across my face, cracks and grays. She tries to write me inside of her story. I try to write her inside of mine. She asks me to leave the past, to walk into a better future, to move away and to make a home together and build a better life. We try so hard to draw each other inside of our stories, and she tries to write a new ending for mine, but the ink goes dry.

"*This, Declan*," a voice whispers, pointing to a family gathered around the dinner table, "*this is what life can be.*"

I catch myself, in the winters and the springs and the falls and the summers that come, getting to that boardwalk a couple of minutes late. One minute turns to ten. Ten turns to twenty. Twenty turns to thirty. I stay for a few minutes less. I don't even get out of the car.

I put pictures of Mason up around the old house, everywhere I can. The house becomes a tomb, more than it ever had been. I stare at the pictures every day to not forget. Mom grows older and her essence disintegrates more and more by the day. Some days she stares out the window and waits for her son and some days, if I mention his name, she looks at me like she's never heard of him before.

Some nights I don't make it to those stairs. I sit in the car at home and try to put it into drive down to Sixteenth and keep the routine alive but I can't do it. I just sit there lonely for the longest time, punching the steering wheel. I study the pictures in the hallway, try to jam them into my consciousness forever. But the face in the frame becomes more and more like a stranger, and my memories grow thick with haze.

It's been over ten years.

Tonight is the last night I'm going to wait for you.

If you're out there, Mason, I am so sorry.

I'll miss you forever.

Warm summer rain, the last hour, alone, the sound of splashing water on the hood of my car. Nobody comes. Nobody stands by my side and wishes me luck. Even Ocean Avenue seems, in this moment, abandoned. How long do you look for the people you've lost? How long do you hold onto a single trauma—how long do you relive it in your head? Maybe it is forever.

"Hey Dec," Mason says, ten years old. "Check it out."

He points to the flicker of fireflies lighting up the summer sky.

I see all of this, this procession of time, soaked to the bone on the edge of the water. I wait for something to come, but it never does. Where do I go now? Where do I take all of this? What good can come from any of it?

When we buried Mason, we buried artifacts—collectibles from his life, artifacts. I haven't been there since the funeral, since we placed a near-empty casket in the ground that day.

It takes me a bit to find him. Eventually I spot a small gray stone with his name faintly scribbled on it, a flood of images from the funeral, roses tossed on caskets.

"I'm sorry about all of it, Mason."

The faint sound of a train in the distance, the smell of smoke on the breeze.

"I need you to let me go," I say.

The stone, cold and gray and chipping away, stays quiet.

"I want to live," I say.

No answers. I close my eyes and try to listen for anything, save the empty air and the sound of a train somewhere in the distance. The breath of autumn and cold hangs in the air, the faintest sound of the earth breathing and colliding with itself on dead grass and asphalt.

"It wasn't me, Mason. I didn't do it. You did. She didn't either. Oh man. Jesus Christ. I loved you—I loved you more than you'll ever know. But I . . . I fucked it up with you, and I have to let you go. I have to live and I have to let you go."

He doesn't answer.

"Please, Mason. Please."

Please.

I am walking inside of my house later in the night. The front porch is lit up and the beetles and cicadas and mosquitoes hover around the front, batting into the lights. Inside of the house, Mom is sitting at the kitchen counter, her hands on a glass of wine, facing me. She looks as if she has been waiting most of the night.

"Hey," she says.

"You alright?"

She stands up from the countertop and walks toward me. She grabs both my hands softly and holds them. Then she looks up from the ground and smiles faintly at me, tears in her eyes.

"They found him," she says.

Part III

16.

"What if I died?" he asks.

He asks the question as a boy. She doesn't know how to respond. How does anyone respond? What happens to a parent when they lose a child?

⚹

The Liberators pick three targets: New York City, San Francisco, Dallas. They say that the pictures that we have seen, the videos, the violence that has preceded it—all of this has been a warmup, and that by the time we move into September, there would be a great Cleaning, that blood would once again water the tree of liberty. These messages are broadcast out the last week of August, the same week that Mason washes up on the beach in Manasquan.

They offer no clear explanation—a strange movement of the tide, getting caught on the jetty, seaweed, whatever it may be—but they find his body washed up on the rocks in the Manasquan Inlet. A band of surfers, late at night, trying to catch the swell adjacent to the algae-covered jetty—these are the boys who call it in.

The world offers equally unclear explanations for The Liberators: perhaps they are bluffing, perhaps there is some massive intelligence operation behind the scenes that will prevent total disaster, perhaps there is no fail-safe and this is how it will all come undone: a handful of shadow figures, hands on dirty bombs. Whispers of violence, schisms splitting out from underneath.

The night they find him, Mom makes me stay home when she goes to the coroner's office. She says she will call on her way home, but she doesn't. When she walks in the door an hour later, there are spots on her face where I imagine tears have been, but when she sees me standing there in the hallway, waiting for her, my phone in my hand, still staring at the picture from the *@mase_314* account, she walks quietly up to me with her arms outstretched and pulls me into an embrace and whispers in my ear that it is going to be okay, even if she doesn't feel it now, even if part of her doesn't believe it, that she is my mother, and it is going to be okay.

She does not tell me what is compelling her to say this, some great need inside, maybe some wound that finally,

finally will get one stitch placed inside of it, but for a moment, in the horror, it feels like something else. My brother is dead. My brother is not coming home. My brother is gone.

"What do we do now?" I ask.

She doesn't answer for a moment.

"I think we need to let him rest," she says softly.

And he could not rest when he was alive—I don't know what it was, I don't think I ever will. I could always see it in his eyes—a churning, a storm behind the flashing marine blue of his retina, as if unanswerable questions sat permanently behind his eyes, poking at him, nagging him. A boy who dies is one thing, but a boy who dies by his own hand is something else, an endless series of riddles and questions, questions that I wonder now if I can ever answer.

Who was the boy inside of this account?

Who was texting me?

I stand outside of Chase's door knocking softly. It is late—nearly midnight. He answers the door and I stand there for a second before I start to shake and he pulls me inside. I am leaning on his shoulder, and for a moment I pull away, but he pulls me back again, says it is not like that, and then I am inside of his shoulder again.

Chase's dad comes down the stairs firmly, stomping his way for effect with each step. He stops at the bottom and stares at both of us. He says something about us. I just shake my head.

"Let's get out of here," I say.

His dad whispers something underneath his breath and I watch Chase shrink.

"Don't listen to him," I say. "Let's go."

Inside of my house later, we're on the couch, videos of Mason playing on the TV. He is standing inside of a cabin, years ago, a vacation to the lakes in Minnesota, his hands on a half-rigged fishing pole that we snagged from a Walmart moments before.

"I want to catch the biggest fish in the lake," he says.

He is just a boy inside of the video, and he is just a boy inside of time now, and on that day, standing on that boat, on the lake, he did catch the biggest fish, as he would tell it, that the world had ever seen. It was a muskie, a pike, spotted and brown and slimy and singular, muscular and ripe with torsion, underneath a Minnesota summer ripe with heat and humidity and mosquitoes and sunshine.

"Why are we here?" he'd asked our mom.

"Because we've never been before, Mase. Because life is out there. Everywhere. And we have to go find it."

We have to go find it, she'd said.

Chase stays with me most of the night, watches videos. He turns off his phone after his dad calls repeatedly. At one point we go to the fridge and he pulls out a couple of beers. It is four a.m., and we are sitting on the couch, still watching home videos of my brother. He says that he remembers when we were kids, young kids, how massive Mason seemed, not physically, a boy who towered over all of us—he would conquer the world, Chase believed, he would conquer the world or he would save it, like some superhero.

"Do you want to watch something else?" I ask.

"No," he says, and I think he means it. "Let's watch him."

It's dawn now and we are outside.

"Nothing good can come from this," I say. The pool heater is on. The water is moving. The crickets sit on the air. There is something new on the horizon, but neither Chase nor I feel it in the moment.

"That probably is true," he says gently.

The air moves between us both, wind rustling.

"But I don't know," he says. His voice trails. "I don't know anything," he says.

At the funeral home, the man sits in front of both of us talking about caskets. Mom explains slowly that we've already had a service, that we believed he was dead, that we believed he wasn't dead, and that we know with certainty that he is dead now. The man stares at us for a moment, surveying what level of truth my mother was operating in, before sighing and saying that he was sorry.

"He would want to be cremated," Mom says. "Whatever is left of him."

"That can be arranged."

"I have an urn ready. I have it ready."

"We have something we can use if you'd like."

"No. I've prepared for this already. I can bring it to you."

"Whatever you feel is best," he says. "We can accommodate your request."

There is a pause, a moment, and the man leans forward as if he is going to say something, some measure of consolation, but my mother leans forward, and gently whispers to him:

"My son is gone. Nowhere now. But I can put him everywhere. Everywhere."

After the burial, the car ride is quiet, the sound of the GPS talking, Jersey air passing through half-opened windows. Mom puts her phone inside the glovebox and clutches the duffle bag with both arms and at some point she fumbles with Sirius until she settles on Springsteen Radio, and she turns up a song that I don't recognize and opens the window all the way and sings softly to herself, and the song is quiet and in a minor key and sad, and the world seems in this moment some kind of funereal toast, some final farewell.

The beach, the one we grew up on, stretches up and down the Atlantic, how spoiled we must have been to move through adolescence in the shadow of something so elemental. There's a soft breeze coming from the north and Mom and I just stand there, staring out at the sea. She wipes her eyes a few times and I watch as she takes her hair out, and for the first time since he left, I see an image of my brother in her face, at least from the pictures she's shown me of herself as a young girl, and what a face—who wouldn't look at them both and call them mother and son, a straight line of love. With her hair whipping in the wind, my mother is, for the first time, so very clearly Mason's mother, and maybe, maybe, maybe, in some alternate universe, in some world we can only sense and feel without ever knowing, they were already together again, and none of this had ever happened, and there were still stories for both of them to tell, lives for both of them to lead, holidays and grandchildren and the smell of summer and the taste of snowflakes on your tongue.

I imagine closing my eyes and doing everything and anything to stay with Mason in my memory, in those instances where he was sick or needed help doing homework or asked me what pair of cargo shorts looked best for an eighth grade date and how I'd told him nobody wears fucking cargo shorts on a date, and maybe, somewhere, if I just focus on those memories, they're happening again, at the same time, in a different place. Maybe the love inside of memory was alive and nothing could kill it, even death.

What I would've given to drill inside his head, to show him the reflection I saw in the mirror, not the one he saw reflected back at himself *("you are not your worst thoughts")*, to peel away the broken picture frames and spiderwebs and raised voices and all that inner churning that frayed him until he cracked and split open. I can still see my mother wiping cinnamon on her rose-colored skirt as she gestured me to come out from under the table, that the bad thing had passed, that The Dark inside of Mason was gone and wouldn't come back ever again. The things that we see as children that just stamp themselves into our brains forever, images and pictures that never leave. What sort of things did I imprint on him before he made that leap? Candlelit dinner tables—pass the asparagus, how was your day dickhead, anything to break the silence even for a second, quiet silences that could've meant anything to a kid. We live so frequently in those what-ifs, those moments where anything and everything could've been different with even the slightest gesture or word, an imaginary sequence of alternate universes where no mistakes were ever made, no pain was ever inflicted, and every word was like a balm that you'd been waiting for forever, like the one where Mason just texted me the picture of his first apartment, where he sits on the edge of the water with our mother and watches the sun set and embraces the magic of the mundane.

But enough.

Mom takes out the urn and walks to the edge. She pauses for a second, opens it, and leans down, but she doesn't tip it over yet.

"He liked the water," she says, almost to herself. "He always liked the water. Even when he was just a boy."

Mom lets him go. Mason splashes out into the wind and scatters here and there, floating in the breeze, the cloud becoming fainter and fainter and the specks becoming more faint. In just a few moments he's gone, nowhere and everywhere at once. Mom stands up, stares at the sea for a while and whispers "goodbye, buddy" before turning and walking past me without a word. I stand there by myself for a few minutes and when I walk back, my mother is an angel, sitting on the hood of the car, a look of something, maybe something, resembling calm in her eyes.

I join Mom and we lay inside of each other's arms, waiting for sleep, the hurt exponential, in ways I never knew anything could hurt. And buried inside of the hurt: the feeling of Mom's arms wrapped around me, the way she moves with me, the warmth of her tears on a shoulder. There is nothing else but the moment I'm inside and I do not think there ever will be.

ꭗ

September 1st

I find Jake on the beach—the same beach from two months ago. He texts me and says he wants to talk and so I meet him on that beach again. The wind rolls down from the north, the summer breeze now slowly turning into that autumn whip, and the air still warm, but with something else inside of it, some measure of change, not quite a chill, but not the same warmth as July. Summer comes and summer goes—and with each summer, some spinning shot wheel of new memories, new griefs, new conquests. Jake is sitting in the sand with a bottle of water in his hand, his feet laid out, the morning sun beating down on him. Around him, herds of families, eager to drink in the water one last time, begin their slog to the center of the beach, close to the shoreline, but not too close, just enough to see the horizon, to stay away from the surf, to put our feet in the sand and vanish for a moment. Everybody dies a little in New Jersey in the summer—every moment is lost in time and in memory, and that creeping feeling with each summer that there only remained so many Julys, so many heat waves, so many melted cones of vanilla-chocolate swirl ice cream underneath the Tilt-a-Whirl.

Jake doesn't look at me when I sit down next to him, just locks his eyes on the water. From the side, his nose still looks swollen, bruised.

"I'm sorry," he says.

"For what?"

"All of it."

"I think I should be the one apologizing," I say.

He shakes his head.

"No. I don't . . ." his voice trails.

"I think we can just let it go," I say. "I haven't even given it another thought, if I am being honest."

A beat.

"I haven't heard from Price at all. I figured I'd hear something. Fucking prick," he says.

"I don't imagine you will."

"Hopefully."

"Have you heard from . . . that account?"

I shake my head.

"No. It all but vanished when he died. Just some scam. Or some prank. I don't know."

"Yeah," he says.

"I can't be the only one," I say.

"To be scammed like that? No."

"I wanted it to be real. I wanted him to be real. I wanted to know that I could have done something different. That I could get a reset, another chance."

"I feel that. I wanted that with that song too. You know what I was thinking this morning?"

"What?"

A beat.

"There was no purpose to it. There was no reason. It just happened. And even if there was . . . some argument that could have gone one way or another, some path in life that could've diverged somewhere else—it doesn't matter anymore. It just doesn't matter at all. It is what it is. It happened. It's over."

Another beat.

"I can't digest that, and I don't think or expect you to, either. I probably will never fully digest that. But it's the truth. It happened. What now? That's the only question you have to answer. What now?"

"I don't think I can square with that ever," I mutter. "Really."

"Then let's just try to take a step," he says. "One step."

"Okay."

"Rutgers doesn't start for another couple of days. I got us one more show at the Pony," he says. "I called Slim. Apologized."

"When?"

"Tomorrow night."

"They're still doing the show? I know places were closing early. All sorts of warnings on the radio."

"Yeah," he said. "Fuck 'em, I guess."

"And Slim?"

"He said he'll be there."

"What a weird dude," I say.

"And then maybe this is it. Maybe this is the last show we ever play. I think maybe that's what we should've done in the first place."

"Yeah," I say. "I think so too."

"You ready for the end of the world?" he asks.

"I haven't even been paying attention."

"Maybe that's the better way," he says.

His eyes stay locked on the ocean. The waves wash up on the beach louder now than they did in July. The water turns in and over itself. The waves are black and dark, impossible to see through. Part of Mason is inside of them now. Part of me is always inside of Mason, and part of Mason is always with me. So it is, I imagine, with love. With loss. With death and dying.

The sound of the waves is like static, harmony and dissonance all at once, and the coming of winter is only a few months away.

I find myself at Lizzy's door on the Sunday of Labor Day weekend. Mom says she is cooking burgers later, and that she hopes I can be there for it. I don't have any plans. I can't imagine being too far from her now. Lizzy has not responded, and when I pull up to the house, I already know what I am going to find inside, even if I hope for something else.

I am knocking on the front door of Lizzy's house and waiting for some sickly figure to throw the chamber open. I sit there and wait for a moment and then I knock again. I hear the sound of the knocking echo inside of the house, the kind of echo that only comes when there is ample space for that sound to travel. I peer inside of the window at the mothballs and scattered wisps of dust on the floor. The family is gone. Maybe as quick as they came.

There is no sign at the front of the house. There is no sign at the front of our house either, the house I come back to later that day. I text Lizzy from the front porch and the message hesitates to go through before the blue text box turns green and the number, much like the Mason account from before, vanishes forever. Her last message to me, the day that we held the service for Mason: *I hope that you find some good in the world—please keep looking, please don't stop looking.*

Inside, I ask Mom what made her change her mind.

"Maybe later," Mom says. "But not yet."

She cries while she is pulling Kraft cheese from the fridge. She says she doesn't know why, but the strangest things will trigger some long lost memory inside of her. She says that she believes these memories will be wounds for days, weeks, months, maybe years. She says that she is frightened for what lies ahead, in both our lives, and the world.

"The cheeseburgers, Mom," I say. "Let's make the cheeseburgers."

I bring out the Kraft cheese instead of her.

She pulls out a foil tray and lays it on the grill and places the frozen patties on the tray. She waits for the tray to heat up and the grease beneath the burgers to begin boiling. When they have melted enough, she places one patty on top of another, a piece of cheese in between. She presses the spatula down hard on the burger, flattening it out. On top, she places razor-thin slices of white onion. She does this with each of the patties and then she hands them to me.

"Place them on the top," she says. "The top part of the grill. Right there."

When I'm done, she shuts the grill and stares at me and flashes a brief smile. She checks her watch and stares back at me and for a few moments we do not speak. When she opens the grill again, the buns have toasted gently and the cheese has melted. She places the meat inside the bun and then spreads the top side with a layer of ketchup and a layer of mayo.

"Here," she says, handing me a plate.

At the table outside, she puts down a tray of the burgers, just four between us, and a carton of mac salad, and a pitcher of iced tea. She asks if I want a beer and I say I don't and she says she doesn't want one either.

"They're good," I say, after taking my first bite.

She follows suit, juice splashing out of the burger as she bites down.

"Yeah," she says. "They really are."

Inside, we drink iced tea and she turns the television set on and the news starts screaming once again about what must be coming, the certainty of it, the horror. The Liberators, since the beginning, have pegged tomorrow, the second of September, Labor Day, as the day that blood will be shed, all will be revealed, all of it.

She turns the television off and asks if I'd like to talk about it. I say that I don't, and I ask her if she'd like to talk, and she says that she doesn't want to either. There is a moment of silence between us before the door knocks, and I walk myself to the door to open it.

Chase stands with his head down, almost looking at my shoes.

"Hey," I say.

"Hey," he says, his eyes still on the ground.

Behind me I can feel my mother.

"Come in," she says. "Please come in."

So he does.

SEPTEMBER 2ND

I wake up on the day of the show, no hangover, but still unable to remember how I fell asleep. The nights are quiet still, the nightmares are still there.

The email comes through at noon on the dot—something I only recognize from the flash on my phone. My heart skips a beat for a moment when I see the sender's name, saved in my contacts: Mason.

I open the email, no subject line, no body, but an attachment.

Inside of it I find the video of Mason sitting in his bedroom. He is dressed in the same Replacements t-shirt that he died in. He is smiling, staring at the camera. The reflection of the camera light makes his eyes look like they are full of diamonds.

"I always, always, always forget to write shit down. And I wrote something this morning, and I think it's pretty goddamn good. I don't have any good words yet. But I know myself, and if I forget this thing later, then at least you'll have this."

There is a pause, and the diamonds go darker in his eyes for a singular moment.

"And who knows right? Who knows about anything . . . I think I want to call it 'Song for the Dead.' I'm not sure why. The chords are easy. Here, look—C, G, Am, F. F, G with the little C thing on the B note, whatever you call it, and then G. That's it. Really fucking simple.

"But I'm riding a high right now and I've written like twelve songs in the last five minutes and this one is good! I don't want to forget it. And I thought I'd schedule this email for the last weekend of summer, so when you tell me I always forget all my good shit, there's some living proof that . . . I do. I do forget it."

He laughs, and then he leans forward in the chair, and the light comes back in his eyes.

"Anyway . . . I have to go though. I'll be back a little later."

He waits a moment.

"And I'll see you then."

The email is only to me. I watch the video again, and again, this one's real, not the cheap imitation of before—a final farewell from Mason.

Then I forward it to Jake, and Jake forwards it to Price. He sends me the screenshot later, Price's last name inscribed at the top.

"Fuck yourself."

ꭙ

The show is well-populated. A few people have some signs. The smell of cigarettes, hot dogs, stale beer. We're up on the stage and Jake passes around a few Solo cups full of tequila and I turn it down. He nods, takes a swig, and Slim is back now, as if nothing has changed.

"It was a good run, right?" Jake asks, five minutes before we go on.

"Yeah," I say, "it was."

On the stage, we work through the same covers. Slim drags. I try to cover it up. Jake turns and smiles every time Slim is a quarter note behind. I just hold the beat down. We work through "Reptilia" and "Sex and Candy" before Jake turns to me and smiles.

"This is a song that my friend Mason wrote before he died. It's his song. Nobody else's."

Then he starts with the chords. I join in when I think I should. Slim doesn't drag. Mason sits inside of the words, the chords, the sounds echoing off the walls.

After the show is over, there's a moment where the stage clears and we're standing by the bar and time just sort of seems to freeze, like I'm suddenly conscious of one of those moments Lizzy talked about it. Slim I say goodbye to with a pat on the back. Jake comes over and says I should come visit Rutgers this fall. He says the football games—the tailgates—are worth it, even with all the fratty douchebaggery. He says that when Mason was alive, all he used to talk about was his brother.

Chase meets me outside the venue.

"It was good," he says. "I was wedged all the way back but it was good. You guys sound good. And that song is cool. It's really cool."

"Yeah," I say. "It is."

"Want to do something stupid?" he asks.

"Yeah," I say. "Let's do something stupid."

Later we are on the beach with a couple of fireworks that we pawn from Mason's stash. We point them out toward the ocean, like we're firing missiles. Each one makes that same wailing screech before spinning in circles out over the ocean. It looks like we are firing shells at the Allied forces at Normandy.

The bike cops make the mistake of shouting before they're on us and we both hit the ground running. My ankle hurts the entire time. I don't care.

X

At home, Chase asks if he can stay over, and I say that he can. Mom is up making popcorn and watching a movie. I don't recognize it, but she says that it's new and that she thinks it's supposed to be good. I ask her about The Liberators, whatever is supposed to be coming tomorrow. She just shrugs and asks me if I want to watch the movie with her.

"And you too Chase," she says, shuffling over, leaving space for both of us.

The movie comes and the movie goes. It does the same thing for me that the cheese did for Mom, and at some point, I have to excuse myself from the couch and go to the bathroom. When I'm back, Chase has fallen asleep, his head slouched to the left enough where it's nearly touching Mom.

"How was the show?" she asks.

"It was good."

"And how are you two?" she says.

"Fine I guess."

"I won't ask anymore."

"Okay."

"You alright?"

"I had a moment before," I say.

"I know."

She shakes her head.

"They'll come and go. Probably forever," she says.

A beat.

"What do you think he meant?" I ask. "I am not gone. What did that mean?"

She shakes her head.

"I don't know. I'm not sure we ever will."

She takes a look around.

"Maybe he knew what was going to happen to him after he died," she says.

"Turned forever into a story," I say.

"What do you mean?"

"That's what happens to the dead. Turned forever into stories, words. That's what stories can do. They allow us things life never will. They let us say goodbye one more time. They let us say sorry. They let us have the conversations we never had with the people we used to love. They tell us the things we know in our hearts but can't quite find the words for, those feelings that don't exist except inside of songs and poems, books and movies. Maybe that's what he meant. Or maybe he was just a boy writing a note on the day he died. I don't know."

She lets that rest in the air. Chase starts to snore. For a moment she looks older, much older, and I catch a flash of her at the end of her life. It comes for us all. When she smiles though, she is the person who raised us, my mother.

I leave the couch without a word, maybe even in a rush, with every word she has said sticking like glue inside my brain, but one phrase more than the rest: *that's what stories can do*.

I step outside, for what reason I am not sure, and then the walk begins, and the walk continues, and I am standing then at the same place where we used to learn to surf, the place that has called me the entire summer. I walk out onto the sand and put my feet in the water. In front of me, the dark of the water, but the sound of something, moving, even alive. There was something out there, even if I couldn't see it or sense it, something.

"Mason, we'll outgrow this place. That's what happens."

"No. I know what love is, man. Maybe it's stupid but I know how I feel about this place, and you and Jake and all of us. This is real. All of this . . . all of this is real."

I stand on the edge of that water for what feels like forever. I don't even know what I am hoping to find, and when I get home that night, the sun is almost rising, barely visible buried in the dark. But it's the light nonetheless. Chase is in nearly the same identical position on the couch, this time just a little more slouched over, his snores louder. I put on some coffee and open up the computer. Then I open the doc with Mason's story inside of it, the one I'd been staring at for months.

Leaning into the Dark

I never liked that title. It wasn't . . .

So I type a new one.

Song for the Dead

There is more of the story to tell—I know. I tell myself however that the ending I can compose now can be whatever I want it to be, that inside of here, my brother can still be. *That's what stories can do,* she says. I've been sitting on it for long enough. So I hesitate before I start to type, the same way I've hesitated each time I've approached the end. And maybe that is the nature of the dead—always past, always present, always dead, always alive. A patter of rain in the summer, the way that the snow falls in winter. The sound of a tide washing ashore. The smell of smoke after the fire burns away.

A flash of text on the screen—*Song for the Dead.*

Mason's story. . . .

And somewhere. . . .

You can see him—he is standing on the edge of the ocean with his feet in the sand. He is alive. Behind your eyes, he is alive. You will need this image of him to survive. You will need that memory of him with his feet in the snow, or the way he held an orange peel in his mouth in that gas station in California, or the way he used to crawl in the covers when he was just a boy or the way that he used to throw a baseball or the way his eyes lit up when he said Mom's name or the face he made when he was crying, the shadow he cast over the doorstep when he would toss his baseball mitt onto the porch before coming inside and the smell of the tar on his hands and the way that he would fold a slice of pizza, the way that he looked when he was sleeping on the couch, you will crawl inside of these memories forever. . . .

Somewhere in between the water and the blood and the sound and the noise you can hear somebody whispering in your eye, "I am not gone—I am still right here, the dead can never die, the dead will never die. . . . "

You will need this image of him when the dark comes again, and someday, you will again find him standing on that beach, beside that ocean, and whisper to him, "There you are, there you are, I have missed you for so long, I have been looking for you for so very long, so very long. . . ."

About the Author

ANDREW CUSICK LIVES AND TEACHES on the Jersey Shore. His work has been published in *Booth, The Hunger, Sky Island Journal, trampset,* and elsewhere, and he has previously been nominated for Best Small Fictions. *Song for the Dead* is his debut novel.

www.ingramcontent.com/pod-product-compliance
Lightning Source LLC
Jackson TN
JSHW081944240825
89232JS00001B/1

* 9 7 8 1 9 6 3 1 0 1 1 0 2 *